Brother Brother,
Sister Sister

Brother Brother, Sister Sister

HELEN DUNMORE

AN
APPLE
PAPERBACK

SCHOLASTIC INC.

New York Toronto London Auckland Sydney
Mexico City New Delhi Hong Kong

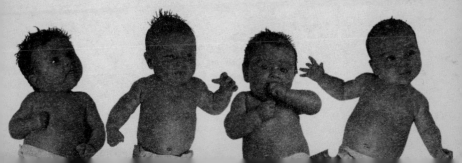

ISBN 0-439-11322-9

Copyright © 1999 by Helen Dunmore.

All rights reserved. Published by Scholastic Inc., 555 Broadway, New York, NY 10012, by arrangement with Scholastic Ltd.

Scholastic and associated logos are trademarks and/or registered trademarks of Scholastic Inc.

12 11 10 9 8 7 6 5 4 3 2 1   0 1 2 3 4 5/0

Printed in the U.S.A.   40
First Scholastic printing, April 2000

Brother Brother, Sister Sister

Chapter 1

I'll tell you the worst news first. Dad's lost his job. He fell asleep at work for the zillionth time, and when Mr. Berger came in with an important client he found Dad with his head on the desk, snoring. Mr. Big Berger didn't say he was giving Dad the sack, of course, in case Dad went to the local newspaper. That wouldn't look good. _"BERGER'S SACKS MILLER QUADRUPLETS' DAD!"_ Mr. Berger said he was going to give Dad some time at home to get things sorted out. _Unpaid leave,_ he called it.

"The sack. That's what it is, all right," Dad said. He put his head down on the table again, in our kitchen this time.

"Rubbish!" shouted Mom. "He wouldn't dare."

Dad groaned. "I'm so tired," he said. "I could go to sleep again right . . . now . . ."

Then the babies began to cry.

You don't know about the babies yet. Let me tell you. I'll just shove about half a million bibs and sleepers off my chair first. And I'd better tuck my feet up because of that

1

diaper on the floor. I *think* it's a clean one, but it feels a bit squidgy. Yuck. Open the bin, drop it in. The bin's nearly full. Four babies times six diapers equals twenty-four dirty diapers a day. Twenty-four times seven equals one hundred and sixty-eight. One hundred and sixty-eight diapers a week! How many rainforests does that make in a year? Having four babies in the house is excellent for my math.

Brother brother, sister sister. That's what Dad told me when he came out of the operating room after Mom had the babies. Dad had a mask on, and a gown and funny plastic boots. He looked like a doctor until he pulled off the mask and I saw his face. He was all shiny and astonished, as if someone had just turned on a bright light inside him. Next minute he gave a whoop, and he picked me up and squeezed me so tight I couldn't say anything, then he whirled me round and round till we were both dizzy.

"Unbelievable!" Dad said. "It's unbelievable! Wait till you see them, Tanya!"

"Can't I see them now?"

"They've just gone into the Special Care Unit. You can see them later."

"What's wrong with them?" I asked quickly.

"Nothing's wrong with them! They're fantastic! They're unbelievable! Two boys and two girls and they're all perfect."

"Two brothers and two sisters," I said, trying out the words slowly. "I've got two brothers and two sisters." I couldn't believe it, even though we'd known for months that Mom was having quads, ever since her first scan.

For years and years I'd had to say "No" whenever anyone asked if I had any brothers or sisters. I remember one old lady in the paper shop who said, "Oh, you're a lonely only then, are you?" But I *wasn't* lonely. I had Mom and Dad and my friends.

And now I had two brothers and two sisters. More than anyone else I knew, and all at once. Brother brother, sister sister.

"Oh, Dad," I said. I couldn't think what else to say. It was all too huge and too strange. Then a nurse came in behind Dad and smiled at us both. It was a very nice smile.

"I'm here to take your daughter up to the Special Care Unit to see her brothers and sisters," she said. I just stood there. It was like a dream where you can't move or speak. The nurse put her hand on my shoulder. She was really kind, you could tell from her face.

"Do you want to wait a bit?"

I opened my mouth but Dad spoke first. "Of course she wants to see them, don't you, Tanya?"

Of course I did. My feet started walking and the dream-like feeling faded away.

I'm going to tell you what it was like seeing the babies for the first time. But not now.

I'm writing this at the kitchen table. Dad's at the other end of the table, writing letters to baby-milk companies and diaper companies so that they'll sponsor the babies and give us loads of free milk and diapers. A hundred and sixty-eight diapers a week cost a lot of money. So do four cans of babymilk. Dad's sure we'll get a sponsor if he writes enough letters. He's got some little photos of the babies which he puts in the envelopes, too.

Tuesday, June 9th

I'm up in my new bedroom. It used to be the spare room, but it was too small for the babies, so I said they could have my room. Dad painted the spare room for me and put up loads of shelves. It's a bit squashed, but it's nice.

I'm in the school play next week, but Mom can't come because Dad's frightened of being left on his own with all the babies. And Dad can't come because Mom is *s-o-o t-i-r-e-d*, and it's not fair to leave *her* on her own with the babies. When they first told me, I wanted to yell and scream just like one of the babies, but all that came out was, "That's OK. Janine's mom can't go either, because she's on night shift at the hospital." And they gave me these grateful looks as if I'd just made them a cup of tea or something.

Janine's mom got her shift changed. She organized it weeks ago, as soon as she knew Janine was in the play. Janine only says about six lines.

I haven't told anyone what I thought when I first saw the

babies. I haven't even told Mom and Dad. Even thinking it makes me feel like the most horrible person in the world. But I'll tell you.

When I first saw the babies in their plastic cribs, I wanted to run away. They were tiny and purple and they didn't even look like babies. They had bandages over their eyes and tubes in their noses, and they looked as if they were going to die. I stared at them.

"Aren't they beautiful?" said Dad.

"Mm. Yes," I croaked.

"Just look at them."

I just looked at them. They looked terrible. They looked like rabbits in vivisection posters. The nurse was watching me and I think she guessed a bit about how I felt, because she said, "It's OK, Tanya. They're fine. They're just small, but they're real little fighters. In a few weeks they'll look just like the other babies."

"Why have they got those things over their eyes?"

"It's to protect them from the ultraviolet light."

"Oh, I see." I didn't really, but I was so relieved they weren't blind that I gave her a bit of a smile.

"Isn't it fantastic?" said Dad. "We're a real family now."

"*We were a real family before!*" I wanted to say. But I didn't.

Chapter 2

No sponsor for the babies yet. Dad hasn't had any letters back, just some free samples. One sample contained a single giant-sized diaper suitable for babies over forty pounds. Dad threw it across the room.

It's the play tomorrow. We're doing two performances, one for the rest of the school, and one in the evening for parents and friends. The play comes from a book called *The Secret Garden*, and I'm Mary. She's really spoiled and bad-tempered and horrible at first, but then she changes. She finds a secret garden with some other children and they make friends with all the animals, and the garden comes alive again. At first I didn't want to be Mary (because she's so horrible), but then Mr. Cochrane said, "Unsympathetic characters are the most interesting ones, Tanya. They need the best actors. I know you can make the audience understand Mary. Go away and think about it."

I went away and thought about it. We'd read the story in

class, so I knew quite a lot about Mary. I thought about what it was like for her to leave her home in India, and come to England where she didn't know anybody. And her parents were dead, too. No wonder she was so angry about everything. If she hadn't been angry she'd have been crying all the time. And Mary was interesting. She wasn't frightened, either. She made things happen.

I love the part when the secret garden starts to come to life. This is how we do it in the play. First of all the stage is dark, then slowly the lights come up, all warm and yellow so it looks as if the sun's rising. All the bare branches are suddenly covered in leaves and flowers. (This is really clever. In the art room loads of children have been working on flowers and leaves made of card and scraps of satin and silk. They've all been stuck onto a big net which gets thrown over the bare branches while the lights are off. When the lights come up, you see all the flowers, and it looks as if spring has come. When you're sitting in the audience you can't even see the net.)

I wish Mom and Dad were coming to the play. It's so good when the garden stops being gray and bare and cold, and comes to life. And they'll never see it. I'll *tell* them about it, of course, but that's not the same. *Oh, that sounds lovely, Tanya. Really nice.*

Mom's shouting for me. I'd better go.

*   *   *

8pm

The babies have had their baths and their bottles and they're in their cribs. I've cleared up the bathroom and the kitchen and made myself some beans on toast. Mom and Dad are lying on the sofa with their eyes shut. The babies aren't exactly sleeping, but the visiting nurse told Mom she was just going to have to let them cry themselves to sleep sometimes. I have put some cotton in my ears but I can still hear them. Crying and crying and crying. Mom was nearly crying, too. Wait a minute, I'm just going to get some more cotton.

10pm

I went downstairs in the end. Mom was asleep on the sofa. I couldn't believe it. How could she be asleep when the babies were crying like that?

"Dad!" I hissed. "You've got to come. They're really screaming."

"I've been up and down those stairs eight times," said Dad wearily. "Just let me sit down for a minute, Tanya."

"Maybe they're hungry. Shall I warm up their bottles?"

"I fed them half an hour ago."

"Diapers!"

"I checked. They're OK."

"Have they got wind?"

"More like a hurricane if you ask me."

"Maybe Mom —"

"No, Tanya! Your mom's got to get some sleep. She was up half the night with them."

I looked at Mom and saw the cotton poking out of her ears. Her mouth was half open and she was sleeping as if a bomb wouldn't wake her.

We're a real family now, I thought. But then I looked at Dad's face, and I didn't say it.

12am (midnight)

I've got my head under the duvet now, as well as cotton in my ears. I was reading over my part in the play by flashlight, but I couldn't concentrate. I can still hear them crying, not with my ears but with every other part of my body. Mom's up again and she's got two of them in bed with her while Dad carries the other two round and round the room.

"Go to bed, Tanya," he said. "You've got school in the morning."

"And the play," I said.

"Play?" Dad stared at me wildly as if I was talking a foreign language.

I've just had a great idea. We could lend them out, one at

a time, to people who want to know what it's like to have a baby. We could call it *The Baby Experience*.

Have you ever wondered what it's like to be a mom
or a dad? Well, now you can find out thanks to
THE BABY EXPERIENCE!

Maybe we could even charge people! I wonder how much? I can't wait to tell Mom and Dad about it in the morning.

Chapter 3

<u>*Tuesday, June 16th, 4pm*</u>

It worked! All the blinds were drawn in the hall. The lights went down and it was dark, and we were all huddled at the side of the stage waiting to come on. Mr. Cochrane and Ms. Burnside tiptoed onto the stage with the net, and threw it over the bare branches. Mr. Cochrane pressed the button on the tape recorder. One bird sang, then another. Slowly, slowly, the lights came up. I walked out from the side of the stage with Paul Harkaway (he's Dickon). We looked up and there were the branches covered with leaves and blossoms. I knew my next line was, "Spring's come, Dickon! Look!" but I found I'd already said it, without thinking. All the little kids from grades one and two sat still as mice, staring. Then someone began to clap at the back and soon everyone was clapping. We did what Mr. Cochrane told us to do when people clap. "Just wait quietly until it stops. Don't smile, and don't look at the audience. Remember you're still Mary and Dickon and Colin, not Tanya and Paul and Bertell."

I hope it's like that again tonight, when we do it for the parents. I hope it's even better. It's hard to believe that tomorrow there won't be any play, just Tanya and Paul and Bertell and all the others the same as usual, and a net with flowers stuck onto it instead of a magic garden.

6pm

How could I be so stupid? Mom was resting upstairs. The babies were all in their bouncing cradles, and Dad was getting the next round of feedings ready. It was just like the play, I'd said it before I knew I was going to say it: "You're the only parents who won't be there tonight. And I've got one of the biggest parts."

Dad had his back to me but I knew he'd heard. He stood dead still with the milk scoop in one hand.

"You *know* why we can't come, Tanya," he said. "You don't make it any easier, do you?"

I scraped my chair back. Everything boiled up in me.

"Why should I make it easier? You had all those babies, not me! I liked our family the way it was!"

As soon as I'd said it I knew it was one of those things you shouldn't ever say, even if you think them. After a minute Dad started to measure milk powder into the jug again. Even with the babies in the room there was a horrible silence. Then Dad said, "I can't do anything about that, Tanya."

I went out of the kitchen. I knew I had to be on my own or I was going to say more things, worse things. I came up here and lay on the bed and thought about how I was going to be really good at playing Mary tonight, because I was just as horrible as she was.

10pm

It was nearly at the end of the play, the bit where Colin's just learned to walk again, in the garden. I was supposed to look out over the heads of the audience as if I saw the robin flying down through the trees. (This is a robin that's very tame and lives in the secret garden.) I had to point up at the sky and say, "*There he is! He's coming to watch you, Colin!*" But at that moment I saw something that had nothing to do with the play. Someone was pulling aside one of the blinds at the back of the hall, just a little bit, very, very slowly. I knew the windows had been left open because it got so hot with all the people in the hall. It was still light outside, so some light came in and I saw Mrs. Chambers looking round to see what was going on. The blinds had to be kept closed, or the stage lighting wouldn't work.

The blind twitched again. Mrs. Chambers got up from

her chair and began to edge her way to the back of the hall. Suddenly a sound cut through the hall. I froze. I knew that sound. It was a baby crying. One baby, and then another. The sound was coming from just outside the open window.

"*Look, he's perched on the tree, Colin!*" I had to say. But I knew what was perched just outside that window. My dad and at least two of the babies. Maybe all of them. Mrs. Chambers was nearly at the window and people were turning round to watch. The babies were screaming louder and you could hear Dad's voice trying to calm them down. HOW COULD HE DO THIS TO ME?

"*Steady, Colin. You can do it,*" said Dickon. I tore my eyes away from the window and tried to look as if a miracle was taking place before my eyes. Colin stood up and walked a few steps. "*You can do anything, if you believe in yourself,*" said Dickon.

"MR. MILLER!" Mrs. Chambers's icy whisper cut across the hall. Everybody heard it. "Will you PLEASE . . . !"

People were whispering now. They'd stopped looking at the stage. The babies screamed and screamed. He must have had at least three with him. I wanted to run away and hide where no one would ever see me again, where no one would point and say, "That's Tanya Miller. Guess what? The Millers have got quads!"

In the play Colin was walking. It was supposed to be the happiest moment of my life. I was afraid I was going to cry.

I didn't. I stretched a smile onto my face and said my next line, *"Oh Colin, I'm so happy."*

But I wasn't Mary any more. I was just Tanya, pretending to be Mary. The play seemed to go on forever, even though I knew it was nearly the end. The secret garden wasn't a secret garden anymore, it was just bare branches with bits of colored card and material stuck onto them to look like flowers.

I couldn't hear the babies anymore. Dad must have taken them home again. I felt as if he'd taken the play with him, too.

In the cloakroom afterwards no one said anything about Dad. But I knew what they were thinking. I got changed so fast that I tore the dress I wore as Mary. It didn't matter. I was never going to wear it again. The play was over. I crammed all my stuff into my bag and ran. But just as I was going out of the door, Rachel shouted: "Tanya! Tanya! Where are you going?"

"Home," I said.

"No, you're coming back to my house! We're all having pizza, then my mom's taking you home. Did you forget?"

I shook my head slowly and dropped my bag on the floor. I *had* forgotten, but I wasn't going to tell Rachel. *"After the play, we'll all go back to my house. My mom's going to cook these fantastic pizzas. Everyone's coming—you'll come, won't you, Tanya?*" And I'd forgotten to tell Mom and Dad. They were expecting me to get a lift home with Paul's mom.

I knew I ought to go straight home. I knew Mom and Dad would be worried, but I didn't really know *how* worried.

Actually, I did. (That's the good thing about writing in a diary, you don't have to lie.) I knew they'd be really worried, and I was glad. Let them think about *me* for once, instead of thinking about the babies all the time.

The party was fantastic. We all crowded into Rachel's mom's car, and someone started singing and then we were all singing in between shouting out lines from the play, but making them really funny this time, not serious at all. Rachel's dad was already in the kitchen putting pizza in the oven and stacking cans of drinks on the table. There were potato chips and nuts and cookies and a big round cake with white icing and *The Secret Garden* in the middle in red writing. Rachel's mom had ordered it from a shop. Rachel's dad toasted us with champagne and then we all started toasting each other with Coke and Sprite and all the other drinks, and clinking cans and saying how we'd never ever forget being in the play. I didn't eat my cake. Rachel's mom wrapped it up in waxed paper for me, and I was going to put it in the freezer and keep it. She's so nice, Rachel's mom. She folded up the paper really carefully and then put the cake inside a plastic bag with a label on it: *Tanya's Cake— June 16th. Keep Forever.*

And then the phone rang. Rachel's mom went to answer

it with her face all smiling. She didn't say anything for a minute then she said, "It's all right, it's all right. She's here. Please, Juliet, don't cry. She's here. She's fine."

Juliet is my mom's name. I felt a red flush creeping up my face. Rachel's mom turned to me, still holding the phone. "You'd better talk to your mom, Tanya," she said. "She's very upset. Your dad's out looking for you."

I took the phone. Mom's voice sounded strange and I knew Rachel's mom was right. She was crying. In the background I could hear all the babies screaming at once.

"Tanya!" said Mom. I never want to hear her say my name like that again.

"I'm sorry," I said. Rachel was looking at me. Everybody was looking at me. All the party feeling was gone, and it was my fault. I wanted to run, just like I wanted to run earlier on when Dad interrupted the play. I wanted to run a million miles away, where no one would ever find me.

But I didn't run anywhere. Rachel's mother took me home. She was nice, she didn't come in. She dropped me off outside, and then I went into the house, and there was Mom. It was horrible. Her eyes were puffy and her face was patched with red. But then she reached out for me and grabbed me tight and said, "Oh Tanya," and the next minute we were all mixed up together, crying and hugging. I shut my eyes and rubbed my face into her neck and smelled her perfume, just the same as it used to be. I hugged Mom so tight.

I was just about to say, "I'm sorry, Mom," when the door flew open and in rushed Dad. He was already shouting as he came through the door. "How could you be so thoughtless and selfish? I've been searching everywhere for you. Don't you know how upset your mother's been? Haven't we got enough to worry about?"

And suddenly I wasn't hugging Mom anymore. I'd jumped up and I was standing in the middle of the room, shouting, too. "What did you do it for? Why did you bring the babies to my play? Everybody could hear them screaming! I've never been so embarrassed in my whole life!"

The louder Dad shouted, the louder I shouted back. I didn't care anymore. It was all his fault, all of it, and Mom's, too.

"Mrs. Chambers is going to kill me in the morning," I yelled. "You ruined the play!"

Dad stopped shouting. He cleared his throat, and said, quite quietly, "I thought you wanted me to come, Tanya. I was doing my best."

I couldn't shout anymore, either. I felt so tired I wanted to lie down on the floor.

"Dad really was doing his best, Tanya," repeated Mom. "Don't you believe that?"

"Yeah," I muttered. "I suppose so." But I couldn't look at either of them. It wasn't worth saying anything to them. They'd get upset, but nothing would change.

"I'm going to bed," I said. I went out of the room quietly,

shut the door quietly, and went upstairs quietly. But every step sounded like thunder. Upstairs, the babies were all asleep. Downstairs, there wasn't a sound from Mom and Dad. Complete silence. Just what I'd wanted during the play, but it was no good now.

Chapter 4

<u>Wednesday, June 17th, 4:30pm</u>

Rachel isn't talking to me. Or maybe it's me not talking to Rachel. I'm not sure. At recess she came up to me and said, "Tanya — " in the way people do when they're not quite sure what to say.

"What?" I said. I said it in exactly the way Mary talks to everyone when she first comes to England from India. Rachel looked at me with her mouth open. Then she reached into her coat pocket and said, "I brought your cake. You forgot it last night."

The cake was a bit squashed from being in Rachel's pocket, but it still had the label on it. *Keep Forever.* I thought about how nice Rachel's mom was, and about the way she said, "Please, Juliet, don't cry." Both Rachel's parents came to the play, of course, even though she was only playing Dickon's sister.

I took the cake and said, "I don't think I'd better eat it now, do you? It might have gone bad." Then I walked over to the bin and dropped it in. Rachel watched me all the time, as if she couldn't believe what I was doing. The cake made a soft sound as it hit the bottom of the bin. Rachel didn't say anything, she just turned away and walked to the other end of the playground.

6pm

Oh, I forgot. A new girl came into our class today. Her name's Natalie, and Mr. Cochrane has put her next to me. She's really friendly.

Saturday, June 20th, 11:30am

The strangest thing happened about half an hour ago. Mom was upstairs changing two of the babies (Katie and John), Dad was in the sitting room feeding Jodie, and I was in the kitchen eating cornflakes, reading a book and keeping an eye on Sam in his bouncy chair. The back door was open, and the way the sun was shining in, it looked like a solid gold bar on the floor. And then Sam started to make a noise, not a crying noise but a sort of chuckling, smiley noise I'd never heard before. I looked up from my book. Sam was flapping his arms around as if he wanted to fly. He was reaching out at the sunlight, trying to grab it. Every time he grabbed he made the chuckling, smiley noise. Not quite a laugh, but nearly.

I knelt down on the floor in front of his bouncy chair, and he flapped his arms even more and this great big smile nearly split his face. As if he was glad to see me. As if he thought I was just as nice as the sunshine. And I suddenly thought something really strange. I thought, *You're my brother.* Of course I *know* he's my brother. Everybody keeps talking about "your two little brothers and your two little sisters." *Brother brother, sister sister.* They go on and on about it. But suddenly, for the very first time, it felt true. Just then, when Sam smiled at me.

And then the phone rang. I jumped up to answer it. At first I didn't recognize the voice.

"Hi! Is that Tanya?"

"Yes."

"It's Natalie here."

"Oh — hi." I'd forgotten that I'd given Natalie my phone number. I don't really know her, only that she's new in our class, and she's sitting next to me. And on Friday afternoon when she'd said, "Shall we swap phone numbers?" I couldn't really say, *No, because I'm not sure if I want to be your friend yet.*

"I wondered if you'd like to come to town with me," said Natalie. "My mom's taking me to buy some things for my room."

"Oh — um — when?"

"Today, about twelve o'clock. We could call round for you."

"Um — no, that's all right. I'll come to your house." I didn't want Natalie to see all the diapers and the baby stuff everywhere, and Mom and Dad still in their robes. Natalie gave me her address. She lived a few streets away. It was only after I'd put the phone down that I realized I hadn't really decided whether I wanted to go into town with Natalie or not. Somehow, it had been decided.

Sam wasn't making his nearly-laughing noise anymore. His face was going red, as if he was about to scream. Quickly, I picked up the bouncing cradle and carried him into the sitting room, to Dad.

Dad's still angry with me about the night of the play. Mom's angry, too, but with Mom it's mixed up with other things. She asked me really nicely about how the play went, and I just said, "Fine." I knew that wasn't what she wanted me to say, but deep down I was thinking, *Well, why didn't you come, then, if you're so interested?*

Chapter 5

<u>*Saturday, June 20th, 7pm*</u>

Just got back. Later than I thought I'd be, but I phoned Mom from Nat's, so that was OK.

I have never seen anyone spend so much money at once. Not even at Christmas. I'll tell you about that in a minute, but first of all I'll tell you about Nat's house.

When I got to Nat's, she was upstairs in her bedroom.

"Nat's just deciding what colors she wants for the new duvet cover and curtains," said her mother. Nat's mother looks perfect, like a picture you see in a magazine. She has polished black hair and dark red lips and nails, and she was wearing a red suit with gold buttons. She gave me a wide smile, but she's one of those people who don't exactly look at you when they smile.

"You must be Tanya. I've heard all about you."

Oh no, I thought, but then I relaxed. After all, Natalie's only been in our class a few days, so she can't know too much about me.

"I'm so glad Nat's made a friend already," she went on, leading me up the stairs. "She's very shy, you know."

Shy? Natalie didn't seem shy to me. But then I'd only known her for a few days.

"Here we are." Natalie's mother flung open the door of Natalie's room. I stood in the doorway and stared. Her room was huge, and it was immaculate. There wasn't any stuff on the floor, there weren't any posters peeling off the wall, there wasn't any schoolwork spilling off the desk. No clothes, no mugs, no magazines. It was as perfect as Nat's mother. There was a thick, velvety blue carpet with a white sheepskin rug on it that looked so soft you wanted to take off your shoes and snuggle your bare feet into it. The walls were a pale, pale blue and the curtains were the same velvety blue as the carpet. Her duvet covers looked brand-new, and so did the curtains. Why was she getting new ones? There were twin bunks with matching duvet covers, as well as Natalie's own bed. Her mother was looking at me as if she was waiting for me to say something.

"What a lovely room," I said.

Her mother smiled again. She crossed to Natalie's bed and straightened the duvet cover, although it was already perfect. "A young girl's room is very important," she said. "I'm sure your mother thinks the same."

I thought about Dad painting my new room. Slap, slap, slap. My dad is a really enthusiastic painter. "Looks good, eh, Tanya?" And it did look good. But not in the way Natalie's room looked good.

"You can call me Toni," said Natalie's mother. "I want us all to be friends."

I blushed. "Oh, um, yes. Of course. Toni." I blushed even more. She looked much too perfect to be anybody's friend.

"Right, Nat, I'll be waiting by the front door in ten minutes."

As soon as her mother left, Natalie jumped up. "Do you want a Coke? Do you want a cupcake?"

"I thought we were going out."

"Yes, of course we are." Nat walked over to what looked like a big cupboard and opened it. Inside, it was a tiny kitchen. There was a kettle, a little sink, shelves.

"It used to be a walk-in closet," Natalie explained. "But then Mom thought it would be nice if I could make snacks up here for my friends." She was opening a packet of cupcakes. "Do you like ice in your Coke?"

I nodded. But I couldn't believe it when Natalie opened a little fridge. A real one. A light came on, and the fridge hummed. There was milk in it, and cans of Coke, and a freezer compartment with an ice tray. Imagine having a fridge in your room. Mind you, if I had one it would be full of baby bottles.

"There you are, Tanya," said Natalie. "But we'd better be quick. Mom doesn't like being kept waiting."

I gulped down the Coke and munched the cupcake. It was amazing. A little kitchen just for Natalie to make snacks in. But I didn't have time to look around properly, because Natalie's mother was waiting. And she isn't the kind of person you'd want to annoy. Better go — Dad's just got back with the fish and chips. I'll tell you more about Natalie later.

Later

Mmm. The fish and chips were delicious. Dad didn't want his batter, so I had it. I was feeling in a good mood so I said I'd have Sam up in my room for a bit. He's lying on my bed now, watching me write this. He's being really good, sucking his pacifier and waving his fingers around. I don't think he knows they're his fingers. I think he thinks they belong to someone else.

Where was I? Oh, yes. Shopping with Natalie and her mother. Nat and Toni, I mean. This is the list of what they bought:

three sets of designer duvet covers, matching sheets, and pillowcases
a pair of new curtains
a set of dark blue coffee mugs for Nat's kitchen
a matching sugar bowl and milk jug

a small sheepskin rug to go by the twin bunks and match the one Nat's already got, and a top Nat saw. (All she said was, "That's nice, isn't it, Mom?" and the next thing it was in a carrier bag, in her hand.)

Total cost: I don't know, but it must have been more than $300.

And it wasn't even Nat's birthday, because I checked. Her mother didn't use any money, it was all credit cards.

Nat's mom (Toni, I mean) asked if I'd like a top, too. I said no. I mean, it cost $50.00! Mom would go totally bananas.

The funny thing was, Natalie didn't even look very pleased.

Got to stop now. Sam's trying to eat one of my socks. Just think, if I had a little kitchen up here I could give him a bottle without even going downstairs!

Chapter 6

<u>*Wednesday, June 24ᵗʰ*</u>

It's so hot. I'm lying on the grass in the back garden. All the babies are in their bouncy cradles, in a row, and they're all asleep except for Jodie, who's sucking her pacifier and making a moaning sound that means she'll be asleep soon. I bet it used to be like this during World War II, when they'd been dropping bombs all night and you'd been hiding under a table or whatever they did, the house shaking round you, bombs screeching and bursting, your ears buzzing with the noise. And then it stopped. The All-Clear. Silence.

The babies have to be in the shade, and there isn't much shade in our garden, except under the lilac bush. Mom's putting another load of washing into the machine. No, she's looking out of the window, checking on the babies.

A funny thing happened just then. I waved at Mom and suddenly she smiled, a big smile. Just for me. I was so surprised that I almost didn't smile back.

Mom used to smile a lot. She used to look really nice, too, even in a T-shirt and jeans. Everyone at school said so. Her hair was always shiny and she had it cut so it swung round her face. She's sort of changed shape since she had the babies. She can't fit into her jeans anymore. And she says she hasn't got time to go to the hairdresser's now. (*Translation: We can't afford it.*)

Of course, I don't want her to look like Nat's mom, with gold buttons and bright red lipstick.

When we go out now, people come and stare into the two double buggies (one pushed by Dad, one pushed by Mom) and they talk about the babies and usually they say, "Aren't they lovely?" Then they straighten up and look at Mom and say, "Must be hard work. I don't know how you manage!" If they're really rude they say, "Sooner you than me, dear!"

As if Mom and Dad *decided* to have four babies. As if they *wanted* to be tired all the time and not be able to go out and have no money and Dad lose his job. When people say with that silly little laugh, "Sooner you than me!" I want to go right up to them and shout in their faces, *We don't like it either, you know! We're not stupid!* But I can't. Mom would kill me.

Another funny thing I wanted to tell you about. I was in the classroom this morning. It was a break, but I was trying to finish a drawing. And I didn't really want to go out in the playground anyway, because I'm still not talking to Rachel and it's so boring, not talking to people when you have to keep remembering about it, and everybody else keeps remembering about it and giving you little looks when you go near the other person you're not talking to. (Does this make sense?) Anyway, I heard someone calling but I didn't think it had anything to do with me. But it went on and on and then finally someone flumped down beside me.

"*TAN!* What're you doing? I've been shouting and shouting at you, and you didn't even answer!"

It was Natalie. I suddenly realized that it had been Nat calling all the time. But she'd been calling me Tan. Nobody calls me Tan. Nobody's *ever* called me Tan.

"Are you OK, Tan?"

I looked at her and I opened my mouth to say, *My name's not Tan.* I wasn't going to say it horribly, just say it. Then I saw a flicker of Rachel's red skirt. She'd just come in with Clare to get something out of her drawer. She was not looking at me in the careful way you have to not look at people if you want it to look as if you're not looking at them.

I smiled at Natalie as if I couldn't see anything else but her. "No, I'm fine," I said, loud enough for Rachel to hear. "What did you want, Natalie? Was it about doing something after school?"

I know Rachel heard. I smiled even more. Natalie picked up my drawing. "I wish I could draw like you, Tan," she said.

I didn't say anything. I mean, you can't really say *My*

name's not Tan, if you don't mind to someone who's just said that about your drawing, can you?

Oh, no. *Air-Raid Warning.* Sam's going bright red and screwing his face up. Time to run for the shelter (my bedroom).

Chapter 7

<u>*Thursday, June 25th*</u>

Hot, hot, hot. The pavement was melting on the road when I walked home from school. I walked with Lisa: big mistake.

"Hey, Tanya, let's walk home together!"

"Oh — all right."

I really like Lisa. She and Rachel and Sushila and I have been friends since kindergarten. But since I haven't really been talking to Rachel I've had the feeling that Lisa is on Rachel's side, not mine. And as we started walking along the hot sticky road from school, I quickly realized that I was right.

"Tanya, I wish you'd stop ignoring Rachel."

"I'm not ignoring Rachel. She's ignoring me."

"OK," said Lisa. "But it's really boring for everyone else. I wish you'd stop whatever it is you're not doing." She smiled, a little half-smile, hoping I'd share the joke.

"Did Rachel get you to say all this?"

Lisa stopped dead. She looked at me, a long look. Then

she just said quietly, "See you around, Tanya." And she went.

I walked home slowly. It was so hot, and besides I didn't really want to get there. I wanted to rewind the last ten minutes, so Lisa and I would be back at the school gate. But deep inside I knew it wouldn't make any difference. I would say the same thing again. There was something in me that wanted to bite and hurt and sting. It never used to be there, or maybe I just didn't notice it.

I used to look forward to coming home from school. Mom worked part-time, and she was usually back before me. When I rang the bell I knew she was somewhere in the house. I always had my own key, but for some reason I liked ringing the bell and Mom coming to the door. Her feet were always quick, as if she was looking forward to seeing me, too. Then we'd sit in the kitchen and have a cup of tea, and talk about the day she'd had and the day I'd had. Or some of it, anyway. If something bad had happened I didn't always tell her. We just sat at the table and dipped cookies in our tea while Mom told me about today's Customer From Hell, and she always made it sound funny however annoying it must have been in real life. Mom works in a shop that sells lots of gifts that are quite historical. Some of them are nice, though Mom says they are ridiculously overpriced, and thank God the customers don't know the markups. Some days Mom would just close her eyes and lean back with her mug in her hands and say, "It wasn't the Customer

From Hell today, Tanya. It was the Man Himself." The Man Himself meant Mr. Featherstonehaugh (pronounced Fanshawe) who owns the shop but never works there.

"Do you really hate him, Mom?"

"Oh, he's all right, Tanya. Just a bit of an idiot, like ninety-nine percent of the male sex."

"Except Dad."

"Your dad's the great exception."

Sometimes we used to tease Dad, calling him the Great Exception.

When I come home from school now I don't ring the doorbell. Mom's got enough to do without that. Besides, you never know when one or more of the babies might be asleep, and it is a worse crime than murder to wake them up. So I put the key in the door and turn it quietly. If the babies (one or more) are asleep, Mom and Dad are tearing up and downstairs with laundry, diapers, bottles, cotton balls, and baby wipes, ready for the next outbreak of screaming. It's a bit like being at war. When there's a lull in the shooting, that's your chance to get some more ammunition together.

If the babies are up, Dad will be carrying one in a backpack and another in a sling, because that way they keep happy while Mom gets on with feeding or washing or changing the other two. If Mom's *really* lucky Dad will have taken two of them out for a walk, and then when I come in she might be down in the kitchen with one baby in a bouncy cradle and another in a backpack while she peels potatoes. The babies still have colic a lot, because they were so small and their digestive systems are immature. Being carried makes them feel better, but you can't carry four babies all the time. I hate seeing them cry and draw up their legs as if they're in pain, and you can't pick them all up because there are too many of them.

I come in. I make myself a sandwich, then I pick up one of the babies, the one that's screaming the most. If it's time for a bottle I give it a bottle. I'm quite good at changing diapers, too, though it's not my favorite job. There isn't any time to talk, and certainly no chance of sitting down round the table and dipping cookies into tea while we talk about our day. And even Mom couldn't make a day with four babies sound funny.

I told you before about how Mom looks different. I wish she didn't. She keeps saying, "I'm sure things would be better if I could get organized." Then Dad says, "We're doing our best," in a way that's supposed to be cheerful.

I hate it. I really, really hate all of it.

Chapter 8

<u>*Saturday, July 4th, 11:30pm*</u>

I can't sleep. I'm at Nat's, lying on the top bunk. I think she's asleep. The lamp by her bed is still on, though. She says she always has it on at night. It's not because she's afraid of the dark, or anything like that. It's just that she's used to having a light.

I can hear the fridge in the closet. It's funny how much noise a fridge makes at night, when it doesn't seem to make any at all in the daytime. And there are other sounds, too. Voices. One of them is Nat's mother. Toni. I don't know the other voice. It's deep and dark and it goes on and on like a thunderstorm growling at the edge of the sky. Even if I put my head under the pillow I can still hear it. Anyway, I can't write this with my head under the pillow. I was a bit worried about bringing my diary to Nat's. It's because Nat's mom is always tidying up all the time, making beds when you've only just got out of them, lifting up cushions and thumping them, sweeping what she calls "clutter" into drawers and cupboards. I'm not really worried about anyone reading my diary, because it's a five-year diary with a lock and key. I always lock it every time I finish writing in it, even though I know Mom and Dad wouldn't ever try to read it. But what if Nat's mom tidied it away somewhere where I couldn't find it?

It would be like losing someone. Like losing a friend. I know that sounds stupid, I know my diary is only a book covered in blue leather, with my handwriting in it. How can it be a friend? I don't know, but it is.

Mom and Dad bought it for me last Christmas. Dad said that they thought I might want to record "an amazing year." We already knew Mom was having quads, though they weren't born until February. I bet Mom and Dad thought I'd be writing lots of little stories about my new brothers and sisters, like the first time they smiled. Or the first time they were sick down my new top.

It's a fantastic diary. It must have cost a lot of money, but that was when Dad and Mom both had jobs. The lock opens with a silver key. The pages aren't lined, so sometimes I do little drawings or cartoons, as well as writing. Like the cartoon I did today, of Nat's mom gazing at Nat's enormous piece of chocolate cake and wishing she could have some. But she can't, because she's always on a diet. In the cartoon the cake is the same size as Nat's mom. In fact Nat's mom is shrinking so fast that if it was a cartoon strip she'd be the size of an insect in the next frame.

Nat's mom bought us a video for tonight. Not rented: *bought*. It was still in the wrapper. We had take-out pizza, and this huge chocolate cake from a white box with a blue bow. I've already told you about Nat's mom staring at it with the kind of hungry look dogs get when human beings are eating roast beef. It was the kind of cake you might have on your birthday: three layers, with thick, swirly icing and chocolate flake decorations. I wasn't really hungry after all the pizza, but I thought I'd better eat some of the cake. It must have cost a lot.

Nat's mom looked at me and said, "You haven't got much of an appetite, have you? Not like Nat!" And she glanced at Nat, a quick sparkly glance. Nat looked away. I thought it was a bit mean to say that, when Nat had just cut herself a huge piece of cake. Anyway, what did Nat's mom buy the cake for, if she didn't want Nat to eat it?

Nat's tall, and she's quite big. She's not fat or anything, but she's not like her mom. Everything about Nat's mom is sharp and sparkly. She has little bony knees. But Nat says she's only thin because she's always on a diet. I don't think she looks too nice with her bones showing everywhere, but of course I don't tell Nat.

I like Nat. I didn't at first, I just wanted someone to be friends with instead of Rachel and Sushila and Lisa. I've never really had just one best friend before. I'm not sure yet whether I like it or not. It's a bit like being in a room with the central heating on full all the time. It's warm and cozy, but after a while you start to want to go outside, even if it's cold and raining.

I can still hear the voices. Nat's definitely asleep. She's lying on her back. I can't imagine sleeping every night with the light on, shining into your face like that. Tomorrow morning we're going ice-skating, then we'll have lunch at the ice-rink café. Mom's given me some money, because she says I shouldn't let Nat's mom pay for everything. I won't get home till about four o'clock, maybe even later. Nat always wants me to stay later.

The voices are getting louder. I think they're in the hall now. That's Nat's mom. Toni. (Only I don't think I'll *ever* be able to call her that.) Their voices are all mixed up now as if they're not even listening to each other. I don't want to hear them anymore. If I pull the duvet right up round my ears — like that — I can still hold the pen. I'm glad Nat's asleep.

Chapter 9

<u>*Monday, July 6th, 9:30pm*</u>

I was going to tell you about our new project at school —
the last project ever. It's our last day in less than three
weeks. I still can't believe it. But I can't write now, I'm back
late from Nat's again and Mom's yelling at me to go to bed
right now because I've had so many late nights. I'll tell you
about everything tomorrow.

<u>*Tuesday, July 7th, 4:30pm*</u>

Sorry, it won't be today. Mom's had to take Jodie to the doctor's. I'm helping Dad give the others their bottles. Going to
Nat's later. She wants me to stay the night but I don't . . .

<u>*Wednesday, July 8th*</u>

Stayed the night at Nat's. This morning I remembered I'd
left my project stuff at home. Ran all the way back home

from Nat's, ran all the way to school, got to school hot and sweaty, fell into my chair, Rachel looked at me, made a little *What happened?* face just as if we were still friends. I made a rolling-eyes face back. *Tell you later.* It was as if nothing had ever happened. I was just going to say something to Rachel, then Nat leaned across and asked if she could borrow my felt-tips. When I turned round again Rachel was talking to Lisa. Realized that if I'd said something to Rachel it would have been the first time since —

I can't remember.

Sixteen days till the Last Day. That's what our project is all about. The last ever project. Lots of people groaned and asked Mr. Cochrane why we had to start a new project so near the end of term. All they wanted to do was sit around with their friends and play games and write cards for people who were going onto different secondary schools, and talk about which teachers we were going to give presents to. (Definitely not Mrs. Chambers after what she said to Dad at the play.)

But I was quite pleased about the project. It's not much fun talking to Nat about leaving, when she only came this term. I can't talk to Nat about all the things we've done since we arrived in kindergarten, when we were four years old.

I can remember it really well. I already knew Rachel from preschool, but we held hands because we were so scared of being at Big School. Our kindergarten teacher was Mrs.

Newton, and the very first day she let me and Rachel give out the milk cartons. Big mistake! I dropped one then stood on it by accident, and it split and milk poured all over the Book Corner carpet. I cried and Mrs. Newton let me sit on her knee. Rachel gave me one of the cookies her mom had given her for playtime. I wonder if Rachel remembers? And Mom used to come in and help sometimes.

That's what the project is about. Memories of Hallam Road School. All the memories, not just the good ones. You don't even have to show it to anyone else if you want to keep it private. You can use artwork and photos and stories and poems and interviews. I really want to interview the cafeteria lady who always put whipped cream on my pudding when I hated it, but unfortunately she left two years ago. I would also like to interview the administrators about why the girls' toilets still don't have proper locks, or soft toilet paper. According to my research source (Paul Harkaway), it is even worse in the boys' bathroom.

Chapter 10

Amazing news! Dad got a phone call from one of the baby-milk companies he wrote to for sponsorship. *They might use the babies in a new advertising campaign!* Dad came out of the sitting room waving the phone and shouting, "We're going to be rich! We're going to be rich!" Luckily the babies were in their cribs having a sleep, as they would have been pretty alarmed by Dad dancing around, shouting.

The baby-milk company is called Superbaby. Two Super-baby advertising campaign people will be in our area on Monday. They're going to come to our house, because they want to see the babies "in their own environment." They reckon it will all be "more natural."

"A bit too natural," said Mom. She looked around the room. There were the usual piles of clothes, half-empty bottles, pacifiers, big bottle of gripe-water, big bottle of baby aspirin, teddy bears, tissues, baby wipes, muslin squares for the babies to be sick on, blankets, sleepers drying on the radiator, bouncy cradles on the floor, rattles, and cans of baby milk (not Superbaby cans, unfortunately — better hide them quick).

"I know!" shouted Dad. "I'll paint the sitting room. We'll take the advertising blokes straight in there, they won't even *see* the kitchen."

"Blokes?" said Mom coldly. "How do you know they'll be *blokes?*"

"Oh, well, whatever," said Dad. "If I go out and buy the paint now, and start painting straight away, there won't be any smell of paint by the day after tomorrow. Just a fresh, clean, natural look."

"Paint's expensive," said Mom.

Dad ran his hands through his hair as if what he really wanted to do was tear it out. "What's the matter with you? This is our big chance! What's the cost of a bit of paint compared to the babies being TV stars?"

Mom looked a bit doubtful, but she didn't say anything more. Dad rushed out to buy the paint. "White!" Mom yelled after him. "Or magnolia! No fancy colors!" She knows what Dad's like. He gets brilliant ideas but they don't always work.

Mom and I started clearing up. Mom picked up a whitish sleeper and examined it, looking thoughtful.

"What's the matter, Mom?"

"I was thinking about their clothes," said Mom. "They ought to be all dressed the same."

"What?" This was strange. Mom's always saying she's not

going to dress the babies the same. They're going to have their own personalities. Besides, you can only get four outfits the same if you buy them new, and most of the babies' clothes aren't new. Mom buys them at "nearly-new" sales, or people give them to us.

"They've got to look like quads for the advertising people," Mom explained. "After all, that's the only reason Superbaby is interested in them."

"Oh." It didn't sound nice, but it was true. Superbaby wasn't interested in Sam and Katie, or Jodie and John. They were interested in the cute little Miller quads.

"We'll go and look this afternoon," said Mom.

"Won't it cost a lot?"

Suddenly Mom looked fierce and determined, as if she was about to go into battle.

"We've got to try," she said. "We've got to give the babies their chance. Every penny they make I'll put away for them."

8pm

Just came back from late-night shopping with Mom. We went on our own, without the babies! At first Mom kept looking round all the time as if something was missing.

"I keep thinking I've left them somewhere," she said.

Mrs. Pearson next door was helping Dad put the babies to bed.

"I've had five of my own. It's like riding a bike, you don't forget," she said. "We'll just take it slowly."

Dad was still covered in paint from doing the sitting room. He opened all the windows but there was a terrible smell of paint. Luckily the babies like it. I wish Mrs. Pearson could have helped on the night of the play. At least Mom could have come. But Mom says Mrs. Pearson was away visiting her married daughter then.

We went into loads of shops, and in the end we got four sky-blue and red sleepers with matching jackets. They looked really good. The saleswoman said, "These *are* nice, aren't they? Are you buying them for presents?" and Mom said, "No, I've got quads at home." The saleswoman looked at Mom as if she didn't believe her. Mom said, "It's true, do you want to see a photo?" and she got a picture of the babies out of her bag. The saleswoman still couldn't believe it. She kept looking at Mom and saying things like, "Must cost a fortune to keep them all in clothes," and "You ought to get a discount." But we didn't get a discount.

After we'd bought the baby clothes, we went into a café. Mom had a cappuccino and I had a raspberry milk shake. Mom drank her cappuccino really slowly, making it last. It was so nice sitting there, just Mom and me, watching the other people and talking about what it would be like if they used the babies in a commercial. I made Mom promise she'd let me have a day off school so I could come to the studio.

All the babies were asleep when we got home. Unbelievable! Mom asked Dad, "What did you do?" and he said, "It wasn't me, it was Mrs. Pearson. They saw the look in her eye." He looked really happy, up at the top of the ladder, slapping paint onto the highest part of the wall.

A really good day. Can't wait for Monday!

Chapter 11

Went to Nat's. She wanted me to stay the night but I told her I had to help Mom and Dad get the house ready for Monday (Superbaby day). Dad's finished painting and it looks really good. The only problem is that having one room all fresh and clean makes the others look even worse. Mom decided we'd have to shampoo the carpets. She's rented a carpet cleaner for the weekend, and we're going to do them tomorrow. Mom and I are going to take the babies out to the park for the morning, while Dad cleans the sitting room carpet and the hall carpet. If he gets time he's going to do the stair carpet as well, in case the Superbaby people go upstairs to the bathroom.

"If they go into that bathroom, it's the end," said Mom.

"No, it's not," said Dad, who is feeling super-optimistic. "If I get time I'm going to clean it from top to bottom. Get all that black gunge out from between the tiles. You won't recognize it."

49

"We'll have to make sure we keep all the bedroom doors shut while they're here," said Mom thoughtfully.

I told Nat all about this, but she didn't seem as interested as I'd thought she would be.

"You can come to the park with me and Mom tomorrow morning, if you like," I said. "We're going to take the babies to see the ducks. Wait till you hear Sam making his duck noises. I think he thinks he *is* a duck, really. I mean, when you think of it, how do babies know they're babies and not anything else?" I didn't realize Nat's mom had come into the kitchen. (Their kitchen is so enormous that you can easily not notice someone for a while.)

"I'm afraid Nat is busy tomorrow morning," she said in a needling little voice. I knew it wasn't true. How could Nat be busy when she'd asked me to stay overnight and then go bowling in the morning?

Nat's mom seemed annoyed with me. She's always been so nice to me before. She was wearing a new green suit and spiky black shoes and she clipped round the kitchen tidying up our plates and glasses before we'd even finished chewing our food. In a minute she had everything in the dishwasher and she'd wiped all the surfaces. It was as if we'd never been in there at all, and I had the feeling she wished I wasn't there now.

It was hard to talk normally to Nat with her mom there. I started telling her about Dad painting the sitting room for the Superbaby people, when suddenly Nat's mother said in an even more needling voice than before: "I'm surprised your parents are even thinking of getting involved with those people."

I stared at her. I couldn't work out what she meant.

"I mean," Nat's mom went on, "it's exploitation, isn't it?"

"It's for the babies," I explained. I could feel my face going red. "Mom's going to save up all the money for them."

"Hmm," said Nat's mom, as if she didn't believe me. "Well, all I can say is that no baby of mine — "

"Mom," said Nat quickly.

Nat's mom was flushed dark red, even redder than me. She looked so angry. I couldn't understand it. The next minute she'd clipped out of the room. I looked at Nat, but she wouldn't look at me.

"Let's go up to my room and listen to my new CD," she said quickly, as if nothing had happened.

"I think maybe I'd better go home — "

"Oh, no! Oh, no, Tan, don't go home! I only bought the CD this morning. You can borrow it if you like. And we can have hot chocolate and I've got some chocolate-chip muffins in my fridge."

I still felt really uncomfortable, but Nat looked almost — I don't know — almost *desperate*, if that doesn't sound too stupid.

But once we got up to Nat's room she didn't turn on her

CD player. She started fiddling with the collection of little glass animals on her shelf. I'd be frightened of dropping them, they're so expensive. One of them is made of crystal and it cost seventy-six dollars. Nat had her back to me. Suddenly she glanced toward the door and said in a low voice, almost a whisper, "Tan. I'm sorry about what my mom said just now."

"That's OK. I only thought I'd better go home in case she was angry with me or something."

"It's not you."

"What is it?"

Nat sighed. She turned to face me. She had the little crystal horse in her hands and her fingers were pulling nervously at its ears.

"I can't really tell you. It's lots of things."

I didn't want to ask any more questions. Suddenly Nat said, as if it was a big effort, "Tan. Did your mom have . . . you know, treatment . . . before she had the quads?"

I nodded. "Yes. But she didn't know she was going to have four babies. They just wanted to have one baby, really."

"Oh, I see," said Nat. Her face was full of trouble. "The thing is, Tan, my dad—well, you don't know my dad. He doesn't live with us anymore. The thing is, he and my mom couldn't have more babies after they had me. Mom had all those tests and treatment but it didn't work. I don't remember it, but she's told me. And now Dad's married to someone else and they've got two little boys. One's two and one's a baby. So things about babies always upset my mom."

I felt so sorry for Nat. I could see how hard it was for her to say all those things about her dad and her mom. And, even more strongly, I had the feeling that Nat could be a real friend, not just someone to go around with instead of Rachel and Lisa and Sushila.

"I don't really talk to Mom about it," said Nat. "But I know how she feels. She always wanted me to have brothers and sisters."

"But you *have* got two brothers now. Well, half-brothers."

Nat shook her head. "Mom won't let me go to Dad's house," she said. "I always have to meet him at a café or the zoo or something. And I don't see Dad much anyway."

"But she can't stop you going to his house!" I said. "He's your dad."

Nat turned away, back to the animals. "I can't upset Mom," she said.

It was all so sad and horrible. I thought of Nat having two little baby brothers she'd hardly ever seen, and of her mom's face when she'd said "No baby of mine."

"Shall we have our hot chocolate now?" asked Nat eagerly, as if she wanted to forget about everything she'd just said. "I've got a packet of marshmallows, too. Let's whip up the chocolate and then put marshmallows on top."

"Great," I said. "You're so lucky, Nat. I wish I had a little kitchen like yours."

Chapter 12

<u>Sunday, July 12th</u>

NIGHTMARE DAY. There are so many bad things to tell you I don't know where to begin. Up early, babies all cranky while Mom and I got them ready to go out. Some of Dad's super-optimism seemed to have faded overnight, and he was worrying about whether to wash the curtains as well as clean the carpet. Mom wasn't really listening, she was too busy changing Katie for the second time when she'd done a poo just after she'd got her clean diaper on. Jodie wouldn't drink her bottle, and John drank all his really quickly then threw up half of it. (Sorry about all these yucky details. Some mornings our house smells like a zoo.)

Mom and I finally got all the babies ready and into the two double strollers. Dad was zooming around pouring carpet cleaner into the carpet-cleaning machine. Mom started shouting instructions: "Don't get the carpet too wet! Don't put in too much cleaner!" but Dad wasn't listening.

"For heaven's sake, why don't you get going to the park!" he said. "I can't start until the babies are out of the house!"

Luckily it was sunny, so Dad was going to open all the doors and windows to get the carpets dry in record time. Mom and I set off with the strollers, the baby bags full of bottles and spare diapers and wipes and rattles, and two Mars bars for us (my idea). It was quite hot already, so we put up the sunshades and then Mom thought we'd better stop to put sunscreen on the babies. This took hours.

"It's half-past ten, Mom, and we aren't even halfway down the road," I said.

"I know," said Mom. "You do Jodie, Tanya, while I do John."

Jodie hated having the sunscreen on. She screamed and flapped her arms around and got a big lump of sunscreen in her hair. She's the only one of the quads who has got proper hair, so it was a bit of a shame. I was planning to put a ribbon on her when the Superbaby people came.

"Right!" said Mom. "Let's get going."

We pushed the strollers really fast, because that usually puts the babies to sleep. Not today, though. Jodie was still upset, and she started John off. Sam and Katie were OK. I really hate going down the road with four babies, two or more of whom are screaming. Everybody looks at you and feels glad they're not you. Still, by the time we got to the park Katie was asleep, and Sam was quite happy gazing up at the pattern on his sunshade. There were loads of people in the park, and most of them seemed to be staring at us as Jodie and John screamed and screamed.

"It's no good," said Mom. "They'll have to have their bottles." She whipped out a rug from under the stroller, and we sat down. But Jodie still wouldn't take her bottle.

"Oh, dear," said Mom. "I hope she's not going to be ill. Listen, Tanya, I'll walk her up and down for a bit. Put John back in the stroller when he's asleep."

Mom walked off with Jodie against her shoulder, patting her back and trying to cheer her up. I sat there with John on my lap. Mom was right, he was nearly asleep. Wonderful. Very, very gently, I lifted him and put him in the stroller. He made a little mewing sound, like a kitten, but he didn't wake up. Very, very gently, I reached into the buggy tray for the bag where I'd put the Mars bars.

"Hi!" said a voice.

I spun round. "You'll wake the babies!"

"Oh, sorry." It was Sushila. She knelt down on the grass beside me. "Are you looking after them all on your own?" she asked.

"No. Mom's over there." I pointed into the distance where Mom was walking up and down with Jodie. Jodie was still crying, but not so loudly.

Sushila was in shorts and sneakers, and she had a tennis racket in her hand. "I've been playing tennis with Rachel," she said happily. I felt a pang of jealousy. First because Rachel and Sushila were playing tennis, instead of looking after babies; second because playing tennis on Saturday mornings was one of the things Rachel and I did all last year. We were getting really good. I liked playing with Rachel.

"Rachel won," said Sushila. "Never mind, my mom says I can have lessons next summer."

Another pang of jealousy. Tennis lessons. *I* was supposed to have tennis lessons this summer. Mom promised last year. I can't remind her about it, though, now that she and Dad haven't got jobs anymore, and there's no money. And I can't stop myself thinking: *I'm good at tennis. I could be really good if I had lessons. Why should Sushila have lessons, and not me?*

Sushila was being really friendly. I just hoped she wasn't going to ask about why I wasn't friends with Rachel any more. But no, she was peering into the stroller where Katie and Sam were asleep.

"They're so cute!" she said. I looked at her. She didn't know the first thing. Sushila is the youngest in her family, and everyone makes a huge fuss over her. She does gymnastics and she has piano lessons, and now she's going to have tennis lessons, too.

"Wait till they wake up," I said.

"Oh, I wish they *would* wake up," Sushila went on, "I want to see their eyes."

"Well, I certainly don't, so don't you dare wake them up," I said grumpily. Then I felt sorry. "Here, have half my Mars bar."

Sushila loves chocolate. We always give her huge bars of milk chocolate for her birthday. But she's one of these people who stay skinny whatever they eat. Sushila never sits still for more than a few minutes. As soon as she'd finished her half of the Mars bar, she jumped up.

"I've got to go. My brother and his girlfriend are taking me to the Lido this afternoon. See you, Tanya!" and she ran off just as Mom came back with Jodie. Jodie wasn't exactly crying anymore, but she looked completely miserable.

"Maybe it's the heat," said Mom. "Oh, dear. Was that Sushila I saw just now?"

"Yes," I said. Then, even though I knew it was mean, I went on, "She's been playing tennis with Rachel. She's having tennis lessons soon. And this afternoon she's going to the Lido with her brother and his girlfriend."

"Oh, dear," said Mom again. She was silent for a while, then she said in a bright, enthusiastic voice, "Listen, Tanya. Why don't you arrange to play tennis with Rachel next Saturday morning?"

"I'm going to Nat's," I said. "Do you want your Mars bar, Mom?"

Now that I'd been mean to Mom, I wished I hadn't. Mom sat down and pushed her hair out of her eyes. She looked hot and sticky and worried. She stared at the Mars bar as if it was a foreign object, and then pushed it over to me.

"You have it, Tanya."

I felt the meanness surge up in me again. "I bought it for you with my own money," I said in a pathetic voice. Slowly, Mom unwrapped the Mars bar and took a bite which I knew she didn't want. The sun beat down. Any moment now the babies would wake and the crying would begin again. I wished I was on another planet. I wished I was in another universe. Once again I wished I could rewind the last few minutes, and then press START.

Later

Had to stop for a while to help Dad clear up. Where was I? Oh, I know, in the park. Right. Well, we stayed out until one o'clock to give Dad a chance to clean all the carpets. We were just pushing the strollers up to our front door when we heard a really strange sound. It was like a small airplane taking off inside the house, getting louder and louder. Mom stopped dead. Then she shouted, "Watch the babies, Tanya!" and she raced up the steps. As she flung the front door open the sound burst out. It sounded like the Concorde now. And out rushed Dad, looking completely wild.

"It's the washing machine!" he yelled. "It's gone mad! It's jumping all over the kitchen!"

At that moment there was a terrific bang, then silence. We all stood frozen, then Mom shot inside.

"What happened, Dad?" I whispered.

"I was only washing the curtains," said Dad. "Then it came to the spin and the machine just took off across the room."

There was a smell of burning. Mom came down the front steps, walking slowly, her face pale.

"The washing machine has blown up," she said.

"Oh well, it was on its last legs anyway," said Dad. Mom turned on him like a tiger.

"*How are we going to manage without a washing machine?*" she hissed. Her face looked as if someone had died.

"I'll fix it!" said Dad. "Juliet, just let me have a look at it. I'm sure I can fix it — "

"No," said Mom. "It's gone. It caught fire. You're lucky the house didn't burn down. There's smoke all over the kitchen."

"Oh my God! My new paint! Shut the sitting room door!" yelled Dad, rushing into the house again.

Cautiously, I stepped inside. The hall carpet squelched slightly.

"Um, I don't think the carpet's quite dry, Mom. We'd better leave the front door open."

I opened the kitchen door and looked in. The washing machine had left its place by the sink, jumped across the floor, and crashed against the table. The side of the table was all broken and splintered. The washing machine door had burst open and there was sloshing, soapy water all over the floor.

"What am I going to do without a washing machine," said Mom again. It wasn't even a question. There was no answer, anyway. I thought of the piles of baby clothes, the sheets and towels, the heaps of laundry Mom did every day.

"We'll get one," I said. "If the Superbaby people put the babies in a commercial we'll easily get enough money for a new washing machine."

Mom sat down heavily on one of the kitchen chairs. "Your father put all the sitting room curtains into the machine at once," she said in the same flat, expressionless voice. "The curtains are ruined and the machine's broken." Mom only ever says *your father* when it's something terrible.

"He didn't mean to break it," I said.

"I know," said Mom.

Dad opened the kitchen door very slowly, and peered in.

"Phone someone. Get them to take it away. I can't stand the sight of it," said Mom.

"It's Sunday," said Dad. "I'm sorry, Juliet. I'm so sorry."

Mom put her head down on the table and Dad came over to her and put his arm round her shoulders. "I'm sorry," he said again.

"The carpet looks nice, Dad," I said. I felt like crying, too.

62

Dad put his finger on his lips. I crept out of the kitchen. Outside in the sunshine, the babies were all fast asleep. Even Jodie.

10pm

Lucky it's a hot night. All our doors and windows are open in a desperate attempt to dry the carpets and get rid of the smell of burning washing machine before tomorrow. I cleaned up the kitchen with Dad. We washed the walls and the floor, then Dad said he'd do the ceiling, which was covered with large patches of sooty dirt from the washing machine explosion. I hate Dad going up ladders. He always falls.

"Let's not bother with the ceiling. The Superbaby people aren't going to look up there," I urged him. "They'll be too busy watching the babies."

"Can't take the risk," said Dad grimly.

When I was holding the stepladder for Dad, the phone rang. I reached for it with one hand. It was Nat.

"Hi, Tan! Have you had a good day?"

"Um. Well. Quite nice," I said cautiously, propping the phone under my chin so I could hold on tight to the stepladder, which was wobbling as Dad lurched up to the ceiling corner to wipe off a patch of soot.

"I wish you'd come with us. We had a fantastic time!"

"Oh — did you?" I tried frantically to remember what Nat had been doing that day. Ice-skating, was it? Or going riding at a new stables her mom had found only three miles outside town? Or shopping for new clothes and then having lunch out?

"Are you all right, Tan?"

"Oh, yes — I'm fine. I'm just a bit — " (I grabbed Dad's leg and held on tight) " — a bit tied up here." Dad slipped. The ladder wobbled violently. "Dad!" Dad just saved himself by grabbing the edge of the sink. The phone smashed to the floor as I caught hold of the ladder with both hands. For a moment Dad arched between the ladder and the sink like a human bridge. Very slowly, he twisted round and took one hand off the edge of the sink and planted it back on the top of the ladder. Then the other. I picked up the phone and shook it to see if it was broken. No! Brilliant! Dad not dead, phone still working.

"Sorry, Nat." I held the phone close to my mouth in the hope Nat couldn't hear Dad swearing. "Um — I'd better go now."

"Are you sure you're OK?"

"Oh, yes! Fine!"

Chapter 13

<u>*Monday, July 13th, 8:30am*</u>

Sometimes Mom and Dad are *so unfair.* Why can't they see that I only want to stay home from school to help them? How are they going to get the babies and the house and everything ready before the Superbaby people come? And then Mom tried to make it sound as if she was only thinking about me.

"Is there something wrong at school, Tanya? Is that why you don't want to go?"

"Of course there's nothing wrong at school! I'm just trying to help you, that's all! Why don't you ever believe me!"

"Of course I — "

Too late. I didn't really mean to slam the door, but it sort of slipped out of my hand as I ran out of the kitchen. Sam and Jodie both started yelling. Even though I'm up in my bedroom with the door shut they sound as if they're right inside my head. And now Dad's yelling, "You'd better go *this minute,* Tanya, or you'll be late!"

* * *

3:45pm

Just got back. Ran all the way home. Everything's all right now — I gave Mom a big hug, and she hugged me back, really tight, squashing all my breath out of me. A funny thing happened with Nat but I'll tell you about that later. Got to help Mom. Countdown to Superbaby people arrival: only fifteen minutes to go! House looks perfect, babies look perfect, Mom looks really nice in one of the skirts she used to wear to work. Dad's still up a ladder (not the same one) fixing the sitting room curtains, which he's just brought back from the Laundromat. Tell you later how it all goes — I can't wait for them to come!

7:30pm

The Superbaby people didn't come until five past five. Yes, that's right, *5:05pm*. They were supposed to be here at *four o'clock*. Mom and Dad had got the babies all ready in their sky-blue and red sleepers with matching jackets. We brushed all their hair (not much of it in most cases) and I put a ribbon on Jodie's. They all had clean diapers and they'd all just had a bottle. They'd all had an afternoon sleep and they were looking —

It sounds stupid, but it's true. They were looking like the

most beautiful babies in the world. Not a single one of them was screaming. Not a single one of them had colic. Not a single one of them had just been sick. Mom lined them up in their four bouncy cradles in the sitting room, and then Mom and Dad and I all stood back and looked at them. Sam was waving his fists. Katie was staring up at the ceiling and smiling. Jodie and John were kicking their feet. They've just learned that if they kick hard enough the cradle starts bouncing a bit, and they like that.

"Perfect," said Dad.

Mom glanced nervously out of the window. "I wish they'd come quickly, so they can see them like this."

The sun shone. Sam started sucking his fists.

"Tanya," said Mom, "just pop down to the front gate and see if you can see anyone coming."

"OK."

There were cars going past, of course, but none of them slowed down. I felt just like I felt before the last school swim meet, when I was in the first leg of the relay race. Waiting and waiting and waiting for Mrs. Chambers to blow the whistle. One car went by, then another. Suddenly I thought I'd better go back indoors. Things never happen if you wait for them too much.

Back in the sitting room. Katie wasn't smiling up at the ceiling any more, she was twisting her head from side to side. And John was looking a bit strange. A bit as if he was . . . *concentrating*.

"Oh, no!" said Mom. "He's doing a poo! He's already done three today!"

"Maybe he's got diarrhea," said Dad helpfully.

John's face was turning bright red, and some very strange sounds were coming out of his diaper.

"*Oh, no!*" said Mom again. "*It's coming through his diaper!*"

"Oh my God, emergency!" shouted Dad, picking John up. Mom was right. A yellowish stain was spreading through the brand-new sleeper.

"Quick, get his jacket off," I said. Mom looked as if she was going to cry as she fumbled John's jacket off.

"I'll have to go and change him. Oh dear, I knew I should have bought a spare outfit!"

"Put the jacket back on top of another sleeper. They'll never notice the difference," said Dad.

Mom rushed out of the room with John, yelling back at us, "Open the windows! Get some fresh air in!"

John didn't look too different from the other three once he'd had the jacket on over a clean sleeper. Four-twenty-nine.

"Whatever's happened to them?" Dad kept saying, as he joggled Katie, who was definitely going to start crying any minute. "They can't have gotten lost."

"I know!" I said. "I'll get their bottles ready, so if anyone starts to cry we can just give them a bottle."

"NO!" said Mom. "They'll be sick if they have another bottle now."

She was looking hot and flustered again, and her skirt had become all twisted when she was changing John. Katie started to wail.

"Take Katie in the garden, Tanya, before she starts the others off," said Mom.

Three minutes past five. They still hadn't come. I was back in the sitting room, walking up and down with Jodie. Dad was changing Katie. John was going red in the face again.

"Dad! He's doing another — "

"Oh, no!"

Two minutes later the doorbell rang.

What can I tell you about the Superbaby people? There was a man called Roger and a woman called Candice.

"Hi! I'm Candice and this is Roger! And you must be the Millers."

Candice was wearing a short pale cream dress and matching jacket, and high-heeled pale cream sandals. She had shiny blond hair and long nails and a perfect suntan. She didn't look as if she had ever touched a baby in her life. Roger was dressed in a leather jacket and cream jeans and he kept pushing his hand through his hair even though it was absolutely perfect. He came into the sitting room smiling and he kept on smiling until I wondered if he knew how to do any other expression. (I soon found out that he did.)

"So these are the Miller quads! Terrific!" Roger didn't seem to notice that there were only three babies in the room. Dad came zooming downstairs with Katie, who was still crying even though she had a clean diaper on.

"I'm afraid they're a bit tired," said Mom, looking hotter and more flustered than ever. "We've been waiting — "

"*So* sorry," sang Candice. "*Frightful* traffic."

Roger was kneeling down by the cradles. "Of course there's a lot of waiting about in filming," he said to John. John screwed up his face in terror at the sight of Roger six inches from him.

"Hi, sweetie," said Roger. He reached out, undid the buckles of the bouncing cradle, and lifted John out. John's legs flailed wildly.

"Oh dear, I don't think — " said Mom.

But Roger had already put John on his lap. John flapped his arms and started to cry.

"Hey, come on now, give me a big smile," said Roger. Suddenly Roger's face changed. He looked down. He looked at John. He lifted John up a little and looked down again. All of us stared at the spreading damp stain on Roger's cream jeans.

"I'll get a cloth!" said Mom. "It's all right, it's only wee . . ."

Roger kept staring down as if someone had stabbed him in the leg. Slowly, he lifted John up in the air and handed him to Dad as if he was a package Roger didn't want after all.

"I don't think it is," he said, examining the stain.

"I'll get the Lysol!" said Mom. "Listen, I'll put your jeans in the washing machine! You can borrow something from my husband. Oh no, I'd forgotten, the washing machine's broken!"

She dashed out of the room, came back with a cloth and the antiseptic spray, and started spraying it all over Roger's legs. Roger leaped backwards.

"Listen, it's absolutely fine, Mrs. Miller. No problem at all. I'll get the dry cleaners to sort it out."

"I'll pay," said Dad. "Just send me the bill."

Candice stood right in the middle of the room, well away from the babies.

"Are they crawling yet?" she asked.

Mom stopped spraying Roger with Lysol. "Crawling? Of course they aren't crawling. They're only five months old," she snapped.

"Hey, that's a shame," said Roger. "A baby crawling race would look pretty cute. You could get some great camera angles. The viewers would really go for it."

"Yeah," said Candice. She didn't sound very enthusiastic.

John was going red in the face for the third time. This time, I was pretty sure it was going to come through the sleeper like spray from a fountain.

"Right!" said Roger. "Well, it's been great meeting all you Millers. We'll get back to you as soon as we can."

And he left with Candice, so fast it felt as if they'd both evaporated.

"Are they coming back?" I asked, as the roar of their car faded down the road.

"No," said Mom. "Never."

"But he said, 'We'll get back to you.' "

"That didn't mean anything," said Mom.

"It just meant, 'We'll phone you later and tell you to push off,' " said Dad. Mom and Dad looked at each other.

"You are *not* going to pay his dry-cleaning bill," said Mom.

"Poor old John," said Dad. He was holding him wrapped in a towel so he wouldn't leak on anyone else. Dad and John rubbed noses, and John gave him a great smile. "*Roger,*" said Dad. "*Candice.* You soon figured them out, didn't you, John? They're a pair of idiots. They don't know what they've missed."

Chapter 14

Later

It's really late. I don't know what time it is. Didn't want to put the light on in case Mom or Dad saw. I'm writing this by flashlight. But I think they're asleep. All the babies are asleep, too, worn out by the Superbaby excitement.

I forgot to tell you about the strange thing Nat said today. I was working on my project, but Nat wasn't. As she says, she really can't think of much to write about a school she's only been in for a few weeks. She's allowed to write about her old school but she says she doesn't want to. I did ask Nat a few questions about her old school once, but her face went all closed up and tight and I knew she didn't want to talk about it. So most of the time when we're supposed to be working on the project Nat just reads, or else she tries to talk to me. I don't say much back, though, because I'm really quite enjoying the project (though I don't tell Nat) and I want to get it finished before the end of the year.

This is what Nat said. Suddenly, out of nowhere, the way

you do when you've been thinking about something for a long time.

"We could look after one of them."

I didn't know what she was talking about at first. I was trying to remember exactly why Rachel and Sushila and I got into trouble in the first year of grade school and got sent to Mrs. Chambers *for the very first time.* It was something to do with blowing up brown bags and bursting them, but I couldn't remember exactly what. I think it was quite a lot of brown bags, though. About thirty. We saved them up. Maybe I could wander over and ask Rachel if she remembers . . .

"What?" I said to Nat.

"We could look after one of them! Like fostering."

"You mean — look after one of the babies?"

"Oh Tan, don't you think it's a great idea? You're always saying how your mom and dad can't manage with four of them."

"You mean — your mom would look after one of our babies?"

Nat nodded. Her face was so serious that I felt a bit frightened. "Yes. You remember what I told you about my mom, about how she always wanted me to have a brother or a sister? And *you* don't want them, Tan, do you — you're always saying you wish your mom and dad hadn't had them. And it would only be one. You'd still have three left."

I felt even more frightened. She really was serious. She really did think it was something that could happen. I thought of Nat's mom with her sharp suits and shiny buttons, her clicking high heels, her perfect hair, her smile that wasn't always a real smile at all. I tried to imagine her holding one of our babies, but I couldn't.

"And we've got loads of room," went on Nat. "I could even make bottles in my little kitchen."

"Nat — you didn't — I mean, this is your idea, isn't it? Not your mom's."

Nat looked at me. I didn't say anything more, but she could see what I thought in my face. I watched her close down, just the way she had when I asked about her old school. She picked up her book and pretended to read it. Her hair slid forward, and I couldn't see her expression.

"Nat?"

She didn't say anything.

"Nat. Listen. Why don't you come over to my house this weekend?"

Nat glanced at me, then away. Then she whispered, "Mom won't let me."

"What do you mean? We're always seeing each other on weekends!"

"She won't let me come to your house."

I hadn't realized it, but it was true. We always went to Nat's house. I'd wanted to go to Nat's. It was like . . . an escape.

"She won't let me come to your house because she says I'm not going to be an unpaid baby-sitter for anyone."

If anybody else had said that I would have killed them. But Nat looked so miserable. She wasn't trying to hurt me, she was just trying to explain the way things were, and how her mom was.

"Oh," I said.

"I wanted to," went on Nat, "but I knew Mom wouldn't let me, and anyway . . . you never asked me."

"Oh," I said again. "I'm sorry, Nat. It wasn't that I didn't want you — I just didn't think — "

"I know," said Nat. "And it was a stupid idea about having one of the babies. I know it wouldn't work. It was just I was on my own last weekend and I started thinking about it, and it was so lovely to think of having someone there all the time."

"They're not so lovely, really," I said. "Not when you live with them."

"Nobody is, are they," said Nat, and there was something in her voice that stopped me saying any more.

The flashlight battery's going. I can't really see to write. Anyway, I'm . . . soooo . . . tired . . .

Chapter 15

Woken up early by strange sounds from the bathroom. Sort of thumping sound, mixed with squelching. Got up, looked at the clock. Six-twenty-one. No baby noise, only the noise from the bathroom, so I slipped out of my room. Bathroom door open, so nothing embarrassing going on. I peered round the door.

Dad was walking up and down inside the bath, lifting his knees high at each step, then treading, down hard. He was wearing shorts and a T-shirt. He didn't see me at first.

"What are you *doing,* Dad?"

Dad jumped with shock, and nearly fell over into the bath, which I could now see was full of soapy water and bulging, soaking heaps of clothes. He grabbed hold of the shower rail to steady himself.

"*Dad!*"

"Oh — er — Tanya! You're up early."

"You woke me up. Listen, what are you doing, Dad?"

"I'm doing the laundry."

Had he gone completely crazy? *Doing the laundry?*

"You're walking up and down in the bath, Dad," I pointed out.

"Tanya, do you think human beings have always had washing machines? Of course not. They'd have thought themselves extremely lucky to have a bath like this to do their washing in."

I looked over the edge of the bath. He'd really done it. He'd chucked all our dirty laundry into the water, thrown in some detergent, and he was trampling up and down to try and get the dirt out.

"It's going to be a beautiful day," said Dad. "I'll have this load out on the line and it'll all be dry by tea-time. Your mom's worried about the washing machine. I'm going to show her that we can manage perfectly well without one."

And he set off again, up and down the bath. I went back to bed.

I woke up again at seven-sixteen. Someone was in the garden.

"Blast! Come here, you blasted thing!"

I ran to the window and looked out. Dad was hanging up the towels and sheets. Even from my window you could see the water pouring off them onto Dad. One sheet had managed to wind itself around his waist. Another towel had fallen on the grass. The line was bowing down under the weight of the washing he'd already pinned to it. As I looked, the line bent lower. Oh, no! It was going to —

The line snapped. Dad's washing lay everywhere, on the path, on the grass, on the dusty bit of earth under my old swing. Dad sat down and put his head in his hands. The sheet was still around his waist, and slowly, slowly, a towel collapsed upon his head. I heard another window open next door, and I knew Mrs. Pearson had seen Dad, too. I looked round for my clothes. Someone was going to have to peel the washing off Dad, quickly, before Mom saw him.

Mrs. Pearson and I picked up the washing and folded it into her laundry basket. Dad didn't even speak. He just walked back into our house with his head bowed.

"Whatever was your father thinking of? Doesn't he know he has to spin the washing?"

"It's broken," I said.

"What, the spin's not working?"

"The washing machine's broken. It blew up. It was old anyway. That's why Dad was trying to do the washing in the bath before Mom got up. To help her."

Mrs. Pearson said nothing for quite a while. She kept on picking up the washing and folding it. After it was all in the basket she said casually, "Tell your dad I'll just run this load through my machine. Not to bother mentioning it to your mother, she has enough to think about. If he'd like to come over about ten o'clock, it'll be all done by then."

I told Dad. I thought he'd be really pleased but he didn't seem to take it in. He looked at me dully and said, "OK."

* * *

4:30pm

Asked Sushila about the crisp bags today. She didn't remember, and said she'd ask Rachel. I didn't watch while she went over to Rachel's table. When Sushila came back she said, "Rachel says she remembers you both cried after you came out of Mrs. Chambers's office. You both hid in the bathroom for ages because you were so frightened she was going to phone your moms and tell them about it."

"No! I don't believe it! *Cried?*"

"Why don't you ask her yourself?" asked Sushila. I looked up and caught Rachel looking at me. I ducked my head straight down again, I don't know why. I *wanted* to ask Rachel, really.

I told Nat about the Superbaby disaster. I didn't want to at first, because of what her mom had said about exploiting the babies, but Nat asked. She was really nice about it. She said Superbaby probably wasn't a very good company anyway. Anybody who knew anything about babies would know that they pee and poo all the time. Only Nat didn't put it quite like that.

"I wish I'd seen Roger's face when he looked down and saw what John had done to his nice cream jeans," she said thoughtfully.

"I'll show you." I did a Roger-shock face, then a Roger-shock-but-pretending-not-to-want-to-throw-John-across-the-room face. Then I did Candice standing right in the middle of the room so her beautiful clothes wouldn't touch anything in our house. Nat was making so much noise laughing that Mr. Cochrane looked round to see what was going on. He looked really surprised when he saw it was Nat.

I didn't tell Nat about the washing machine disaster, though. Her mom's got a special room for washing, called a utility room. It's got a huge washing machine and a spin-dryer and a tumble-dryer, as well as a sink for washing the stuff that's too wonderful to go into a machine. I didn't really want to do Dad for Nat, with him trampling up and down the bath then sitting on the lawn with all the sheets and towels collapsing all over him. Even though it was funny.

6:30pm

Unbelievable news! Mrs. Pearson's just been round to talk to Mom. She didn't say anything at all about the washing business. (Dad had already told me he'd fetched the clean laundry at ten this morning, and so Mom never knew anything about the washing-in-the-bath episode.) Mrs. Pearson said to Mom that her married daughter was having a new kitchen put in, and she was having everything custom made, so she was getting rid of her old equipment. She had an old washing machine she didn't want. Would Mom like it as backup? It had a year or two of life in it still, and if Mom didn't want it, it would just go for scrap. Mom went very pale, and held onto the door handle. When she answered her voice was squeaky.

"Oh, Mrs. Pearson, I can't believe it. You won't believe it, either, when I tell you what happened to our washing machine yesterday. The motor exploded and it can't be mended. This is like a gift from heaven."

"Well, my daughter will be very grateful to anyone who can take it off her hands," said Mrs. Pearson. "As it happens she's got a man with a van coming tomorrow to clear out some other stuff, so he can bring the machine along for you then. About eleven o'clock?"

I saw Mom's face when she came back from saying goodbye to Mrs. Pearson at the door. Her eyes were full of tears. I looked away quickly so she wouldn't see that I'd seen.

Chapter 16

Dad's gone out.

"Where are you going, Dad?"

"Nowhere. Just out."

I nearly asked if I could come with him. A year ago I would have, and he'd have turned round and smiled and said, "OK, get your jacket." Dad and I used to go off on long walks together sometimes, nowhere special, just wandering. Looking into shops, maybe going into a café and having a huge hot chocolate with toasted marshmallows on the top, or a hot fudge sundae. Dad loved looking round the markets. He was always picking up bargains — at least, that's what he called them, though Mom wasn't so sure. But she didn't mind then. We used to have more money then, when they were both working, so it didn't matter so much about every single quarter you spent.

Used to. We always used to. That's how old people talk when they're talking about things that happened fifty years ago. Maybe I'm thinking like this because our school project is all about the past. And not other people's past, like the Romans or the Victorians, but *our* past. The past I remember. All those things we used to do: double Dutch and Mother May I and all the games you forget about as soon as you're too old to go on playing them.

I remember one little red jacket I used to have. It had a hood with little red strings to pull it tight, and Mom bought me some matching red gloves. I loved my red jacket so much that I kept on wearing it even when the weather was warm. I used to tell myself all sorts of stories about how it was a magic jacket and I could make myself invisible in it. Then, the next winter, I had a really dull navy-blue jacket, and I kept putting on the old red one, even though it was much too small and the zipper was broken.

This morning was awful. Mom was happy because of the washing machine coming at eleven o'clock, but Dad just sat at the kitchen table tearing up the whole file of stuff he'd collected about firms that might sponsor the babies, or give us loads of money for putting them in commercials.

"Aren't you going to write to them anymore?" I asked.

"Waste of time," said Dad. Gloom hung around him so heavily that I wouldn't have been surprised if it had started raining inside the kitchen. Katie and Sam were lying on the rug, trying to roll over, but Dad didn't even look at them. Gloom everywhere. Maybe we could start a gloom factory. I must have smiled without realizing it, because Dad snapped, "I don't know why you think it's so funny, Tanya. Time's money, you know."

Time's money. It really annoyed me. *Time is time,* I wanted to shout. *Why do you keep on wasting it, being so gloomy?* But I didn't say anything. I just escaped to school.

"Come to my house after school? *Please!* My mom's going out."

"I can't always come to your house, Nat. You've got to start coming to mine." Then I thought of the Gloom Factory I'd left that morning. No, maybe not. "Oh, OK, I mean, thanks Nat, I'd like to."

"Oh, good. Mom's going to get back late, and I don't really like being on my own."

I remembered to phone home. Dad answered. As soon as I heard his voice I could tell that the Gloom Factory had been in full production all morning, even though Mom was yelling in the background, "Tell her the washing machine's arrived, and it's working!" I put down the phone, feeling glad I was going to Nat's.

I forgot to tell you about something important which happened at school, just before lunch. Sushila came over again and sat on my table.

"Tanya?"

"Mm." I was busy drawing a picture of me and Rachel hiding in the girls' bathroom crying. I was also wishing we'd had one of those disposable cameras all the way through our time at Hallam Road. We could have made a brilliant scrapbook.

"Tanya, Rachel's writing something about the newspaper we started in Mrs. Fontana's class. Have you still got a copy of it anywhere?"

I knew I had. I knew exactly where it was — in the third drawer down in my little chest of drawers, where I put all the drawings and letters and stuff that I want to keep.

"Hasn't she got one?"

"No. She thinks her mom threw it away by mistake."

It sounds funny, but it was quite a relief to think that Rachel's mom could have done a thing like that. Rachel's mom does such fantastic parties, and makes delicious cakes when you go round to tea, and always looks so nice. It's good to know she isn't perfect.

"I think I might have got it somewhere," I said to Sushila. "I'll have a look tonight and bring it in tomorrow. Tell Rachel."

Sushila gave me a big, sparkling smile, and skipped off back to tell Rachel. I sat smiling too, staring into space, feeling good. Nearly as good as I'd felt before, when I was being mean, to tell you the truth.

It was great at Nat's, especially since her mother wasn't there. We cooked our own meal — chicken pieces, french fries, and frozen peas, followed by lemon meringue pie and ice cream. (Nat's mom had left the pie in the fridge for us, still in its expensive baker's box.) We tried on some of Nat's mom's jewelry, which was a bit frightening because I kept listening for the sound of her key in the door and her sharp heels coming clickety-click across the wooden hall floor. (This is not the kind of wooden floor you have when you can't afford a carpet so you just polish up the floorboards a bit. It's the kind that a team of four experts comes in to lay, and it takes more than a week, and it cost *more than fifteen hundred dollars*. Nat told me.)

Nat says she always tries on her mom's jewelery when her mom's out of the house. There is a huge box full of it, with little sliding drawers for rings, brooches, earrings, and bracelets. She has separate boxes for her necklaces. All the jewelry is sharp and shiny and prickling-looking, like Nat's mom. Nat knows the names of all the stones in the brooches and rings. I didn't really enjoy looking at it all that much.

After that Nat wanted us to look at her mom's clothes, but I didn't want to, so I suggested we watch a video. I could see why Nat didn't really like being in the house on her own. Upstairs, the carpets are so thick that your feet hardly make any noise at all. A burglar could easily come creeping up behind you before you knew he was there. And it's so quiet you can hear the clocks tick when you open the doors to the rooms.

It was a long video. I didn't realize how late it was until

suddenly I saw it was getting dark. Nat's mom still hadn't come home, though it was half-past nine.

"Don't go yet, Tan," Nat said. "Let's have another Coke. Or I could cook us some pizza slices. Mom said we could have anything we wanted."

"I've got to go, Nat. I told Dad I wouldn't be late."

I suddenly remembered that I'd also told Dad that Nat's mom would be bringing me home.

"Nat, do you know what time your mom's coming back?"

Nat shook her head.

"I mean, do you think she'd mind giving me a lift?"

"She might not be back for ages," said Nat. "She always says to me just to go to bed and not wait up for her. Listen, Tan, you can stay the night. You can sleep in my room. I've got loads of spare nighties."

Nat sounded really eager. It seemed so mean, to leave her on her own when she was frightened of being alone in the house.

"I'm sorry, Nat. I've got to go home. But you could come back with me if you want. Just leave a note for your mom."

"I can't do that," said Nat quickly. I remembered the "unpaid baby-sitter" bit and I felt angry again. Not with Nat, not really . . . But why did Nat always do as her mother told her, no matter how stupid it was?

I thought about phoning Dad to ask him to walk round and fetch me, then I remembered the Gloom Factory. I could run back. I'd run so fast I'd be home in less than five minutes. There were only a few streets between my house and Nat's. But it was getting darker and darker. I'd have to go right away.

I raced down Nat's street, and turned into the next, where the houses started getting smaller. The cars had their head-lights on. I kept seeing the frightened look on Nat's face. I wished I'd stayed — but I couldn't stay, could I? Down the street, across the road, into the next, running hard, hearing the thump of my feet on the night pavement. I was at the gate. I slowed down, and fumbled in my jeans pocket for my door key.

"Is that you, Tanya? I didn't hear a car."

"Oh — Nat's mom dropped me a little way down the road, so she could turn the car — round."

Dad came out of the kitchen, frowning. "She should see you right to the front door, when it's as late as this."

"Oh, she was watching me from the car."

I didn't even go red. Lying was getting as easy for me as being mean. I looked straight at Dad, smiling. He looked awful. Tired and worried and crumpled up. He had Jodie in the backpack.

"Colic," he said hopelessly. "Or maybe she's started

teething. Do you think babies can go straight from colic to teething, Tanya?"

"I don't know," I said. "I've got to write in my diary." And I escaped upstairs. Dad is doing overtime in the Gloom Factory tonight.

Chapter 17

<u>Thursday, July 16th, 8:30pm</u>

Went to Nat's after school. Remembered to phone home and tell Mom and Dad, so I don't know why they were both so grumpy when I got back. Just a minute — I've got to go and phone Nat and tell her it's OK about Saturday. TENNIS LESSONS! Nat's mom has arranged it all. Mom says it's OK.

<u>9:30pm</u>

As soon as I went downstairs, Dad started.
Dad: Why are you on the phone with that girl — what's her name — when you only left her house five minutes ago?
Me: Her name is Nat. Natalie. I'm calling her because I want to talk to her.
Dad: (*rocking Katie so hard her head bobbles against his shoulder*) Don't you talk to me like that, young lady!
Me: Be careful with Katie, Dad!

Dad: And what's all this you were telling your mother about tennis lessons?

Me: (*a bit nervously, because when Dad says "your mother" it is definitely bad news*) Um — well, Nat's having tennis lessons on Saturdays, and her mother asked if I'd like to share them.

Dad: Who's paying?

Me: Um — er — I don't know.

Dad: JULIET! Who is paying for these tennis lessons Tanya says she's going to have?

Mom: (*appearing from the kitchen looking flustered*) Oh dear, I think it's all right, love. Apparently this Natalie needs a partner, so they asked if Tanya would like to go along.

Dad: You mean *she's* paying? This whoever-her-name-is, Natalie's mother? The one who doesn't bother to bring my daughter back to the front door when she gives her a lift home?

Mom: Oh, Alan.

Dad: Well, I'm not having it. No one in my family is having any blasted charity from anybody. Tanya can just telephone her friend and tell her the tennis lessons are *off*.

Me: DAD!

Mom: Be quiet, Tanya. Now, Alan, listen. It's not charity. It's for Natalie's sake as much as for Tanya's.

Dad: (*pacing up and down the floor like a tiger*) Don't talk to *me* about charity. I wasn't born yesterday. Where did that washing machine come from?

Mom: For heaven's sake, you know where it came from! Mrs. Pearson's married daughter was doing her kitchen and she didn't want it —

Dad: A likely story! You must think I'm an idiot!

Mom: (*really angry now, too*) Don't you talk to me about washing machines! Who was it who blew up our washing machine?

Dad: OK. All right. We keep the washing machine. I'll put up with the washing machine. BUT TENNIS LESSONS, NO! Over my dead body.

Me: (*sliding round the door on my way out*) I think I'll just go round to Natalie's for half an hour, Mom, I've got to talk to her about my school project.

Mom and Dad together: YOU ARE NOT GOING ANY-WHERE AT THIS TIME OF NIGHT, TANYA!

10:20pm

Mom's just been up. She knocked really softly at my door, so I pretended not to notice, but then she came in anyway.

"Tanya?"

"Mm?"

"Tanya, you mustn't mind what your dad said. He's upset, that's all."

"You *said* I could have tennis lessons with Nat."

"I know. But maybe — maybe we could leave it just a week or two, love? Let your dad get over all this."

I looked at Mom. I wanted to wrap my arms tight around her and shut my eyes and wait for her to make everything all right again, the way she used to do. But I didn't. I just nodded.

"OK, Mom."

"Oh, Tanya, I'm sorry. It's a difficult time. Maybe when Dad gets another job . . ."

I pressed my lips tight together. If we started to talk about Dad or jobs or money or tennis lessons I was going to cry. Mom looked at me in a hopeful sort of way for a minute, then slowly she got up from where she'd sat down on my bed.

"Night, Tanya."

"Night, Mom."

_11:30pm_

I forgot to say — I gave Rachel the newspaper we did in Mrs. Fontana's. Tell you more in the morning.

Chapter 18

Friday, July 17th

It's really early. Going to be another hot day. Mom's up — I can hear her in the babies' room. But I'm not going to get out of bed yet.

I meant to tell you yesterday about giving Rachel the class newspaper. I found it in my drawer. It was in a plastic folder, and suddenly I remembered Mom giving me the folder and a label and saying, "It won't get creased if you put it away in this. You'll be glad you've kept it when you're older, Tanya."

She was right. I took the newspaper out of the folder. We'd done it on the computer at school, but underneath the computer version there was the handwritten one, the original one with all the little drawings we'd done. My handwriting was completely different then. I remember how we wrote all the articles out in our best handwriting, then cut-and-pasted them onto big sheets of plain white paper, along with the drawings. Mrs. Fontana was so pleased that she said we could use the school computer, and then we'd be able to make lots of copies, for everyone in the class.

The drawings are so funny. I remember Rachel doing the one of Mrs. Fontana running in the Teachers' Race on Sports Day. Her legs are flying up in the air and she is dropping banana skins behind her so all the other teachers slide and skid and fall over. There's a balloon coming out of her mouth saying, "Out of my way, Earthlings! I am the victor!" Then there's a long article about the great disaster when a cat got through the fence into the wildlife garden. It ate all the tadpoles in our school pond, just as they were turning into frogs. *Metamorphosing*. I remember Mrs. Fontana writing that word on the board for us. There's a picture of the great cat disaster. The cat's licking his whiskers, looking sleek and satisfied, beside a little row of gravestones with *RIP Tadpoles* written along it, one letter on each gravestone. It was Paul Harkaway who did that. It's quite a good newspaper, really, when you think that we were just little third grade kids.

I took the whole folder into school to show Rachel. Not just the computer version, but the handwritten one, too. I knew Rachel would remember us doing it, just as I did. Just before recess I went over to the table where Rachel and Lisa and Sushila were sitting. Lisa looked up. Her face wasn't particularly friendly.

"Hi," I said as casually as I could. "I've brought the newspaper we did in Mrs. Fontana's. It's all in this folder."

Rachel's face changed. It really did light up, just like people say in books. She looked at me, then at the folder, then she undid the little plastic button which closed it, and drew out the sheets of the newspaper. First the computer version, then the handwritten one.

"Wow! I didn't realize you'd kept all this!"

"I said I would. Don't you remember?"

Rachel was turning over the pages. "There's your cartoon, Sushila! Oh, look — didn't we all have pathetic handwriting?"

"Yeah — but look, have you seen Paul's drawing of the tadpole cemetery? It's really good."

"I can't believe we did all this."

We were all leaning over the table, poring over the newspaper. Suddenly I had the strangest feeling, as if time had slipped back and we were in Mrs. Fontana's again, all excited over the newspaper, all doing our articles and drawings and cartoons, all incredibly thrilled when we'd pasted them together and it started looking like a proper newspaper (well, we thought it looked like a proper newspaper then. . .). The bell for recess rang, but I hardly noticed it.

"Do you remember how — "

"Hey, who did this one! It's really good!"

"Oh my God, I'd forgotten about this drawing of Mrs. Chambers! Doesn't she look like a witch?"

"She *is* a witch."

Then I glanced round. There was Nat, staring over at us.

She looked as if she was lost, far away from home, and she didn't know how to get back. Then she looked down, quickly, pretending to read her library book.

"You can keep the newspaper till you've finished your project," I said to Rachel. "But make sure you keep it in the folder."

"I don't see why it's *your* newspaper, any more than Rachel's," said Lisa. "After all, we all worked on it."

But Rachel said, "Tanya's looked after it ever since third grade. If I'd had it, my mom would have thrown it away, just like she threw away the computer one. She's a tidiness maniac! Thanks, Tanya."

"S'OK."

I moved away from the circle around the newspaper. Nat was reading hard, her head bent low over the book so I couldn't see her face.

"Nat?"

"What?"

"Coming out to the playground?"

Nat looked up, keeping her finger on her place. "Don't you want to go with Rachel and Lisa and Sushila?"

"They're not going out. They're working on their projects."

Slowly, Nat got up. "D'you want half my Twix, Tanya? Or you can have a whole one if you like. My mom gave me two."

"No," I said. "Listen. I've got a Mars bar. You have half of mine."

"It's OK, Tanya! I've got two, really!"

"Nat, *I want to share my Mars bar with you.* I don't always want to be taking your stuff. I mean, that's not what friends do."

Nat glanced quickly at me, then away. Her hair swung forward again, but this time I could see she was smiling. Suddenly it hit me. *She hadn't called me Tan!* For the first time, Nat had called me Tanya. Twice. Just like all my other friends.

Mom's calling. The babies are all crying. Dad's just gone thundering down the stairs. Time to escape to school!

Oh, no. I've just realized. There is only one more week left until the end of the year. Six weeks of vacation.

Tanya, can you just take Katie —

Tanya, make some more bottles, there's a good girl —

Tanya, your mom's worn out. Bring the washing in for her —

Tanya, can you tidy up the kitchen? It looks like a bomb's hit it —

Six weeks. Get out the calculator. That makes . . . let me see . . . one thousand and eight bottles, and one thousand and eight dirty diapers!

Mom's really yelling now. Got to go!

Chapter 19

Friday, July 17th, 4:30pm

Great news! *Dad has got a job*. He's going to do all the book-keeping for the Chinese supermarket in Whitehorse Road. He's starting next week. They want him to go in every Saturday and do about eight hours. Dad says they're really behind with all their bookkeeping, so there's loads of work. He'll be there for at least two months, maybe more. It might even be permanent. Dad says that this is just the start. They might recommend him to other businesses. And the best part is, with this kind of thing he can work evenings and weekends, and help Mom with the babies during the week. It's perfect.

The Chinese supermarket is going to pay Dad thirteen dollars an hour! Thirteen times eight is one hundred four. One hundred four extra dollars a week coming into the house. And Dad says they've said they'll raise it to fifteen dollars an hour after the first month.

More great news! I'm going to Mere Park with Nat next Saturday, to celebrate the end of the school year. They have the best roller-coasters in the whole country at Mere Park. And Mom says she can manage the babies on her own, just for one Saturday. I've promised I'll help her on the other Saturdays, when Dad's working. And Dad says he'll give me extra pocket money for helping out on Saturdays. "After all, Tanya," he said, "I wouldn't be able to do the job if you weren't here to help Mom." Haven't asked him how much extra yet.

And the best news of all is that the Gloom Factory has gone out of production.

Monday, July 20th

I've been too busy to write. Went to Nat's on Saturday — went skating — helped Nat choose a new bookshelf for her room. We spent ages just looking in shops.

Worked on the project nearly all today. It's almost finished. We read parts aloud today, to the rest of the class — only people who wanted to read. I didn't really want to. The project feels a bit like a diary — something you do for yourself, not for other people. But I loved the bit Sushila read, about when she climbed to the top of the climbing wall on a dare, then climbed right onto the very top platform and up onto the window frame (one of those huge, high windows in the gym) — and then got stuck and couldn't climb down again. And we were all nearly crying because we knew they'd find out we'd dared her. And Rachel kept saying, "She's going to die and it's all our fault!"

Tuesday, July 21st

Only three more days to go until the Last Day. The last day ever at Hallam Road School. Hardly anyone is doing any work now. We had a concert today, and a kind of graduation speech from Mrs. Chambers (nightmare!). I'm still trying to finish the project — trying to get it right up to date. Tomorrow I'm going to bring in Mom's camera and take photos of everybody, then stick them in the project afterwards. I'm even going to take photos of people I don't like—just for the record.

Wednesday, July 22nd

Took loads of photos. Everybody in our class, the cafeteria ladies, all the teachers I've had who are still here, Mrs. Osmond (the school secretary) — everybody. I asked if I could go into the kindergarten class and photograph the little ones. I'm going to put that photo on the very last page, and write *The Next Generation* under it. I can't believe we were ever that small. All the kindergarten kids sat on the Book Corner carpet for me to take the photograph. I had a sudden, vivid memory of the milk I'd spilt all over that carpet, and how frightened I was. Big School, and I'd blown it on the very first day.

They sat really still, all crammed together. *Click!* Then they jumped up and went off to play, or do whatever it is they do. I had the strangest thought. Although they'd been sitting on the carpet in the Book Corner only about a minute before, it was already history. It was just as much history as me being in kindergarten myself. It would never happen again. But I didn't have time to really think about it. There was too much going on.

Thursday, July 23rd

Tomorrow is the Last Day. Graduation party in the afternoon. I feel so tired. I won't write any more, I'm just going to stick the last drawings and stuff into my project. Then I've got to give Sam and Katie a bath.

Friday, July 24th

It's over. It's all over. People were running around the school crying and saying goodbye to everyone and swapping phone numbers and saying how we'd never forget each other even if we were going onto different schools. It was crazy. We went around to all the classrooms to say goodbye to the teachers and, every time, somebody started crying. The party was awful. I just wanted to go home. Rachel and Sush and I cut up the graduation cake Rachel's mom had made. Nat kept sort of disappearing into the background, as if it wasn't her party at all. I kept saying to her, "Nat, you're graduating just as much as anybody else!" but she just shook her head.

And then it was over. The bell rang. It sounds stupid, but it was only at that moment that I realized I wouldn't ever hear the bell again, or get my stuff out of my drawer and put it in my backpack, or get my jacket, and say "See you tomorrow!" to my friends. It was all over. We all went out together, some of us throwing books and jackets and backpacks into the air, others holding onto their best friends and crying. I could already hear the janitors banging their buckets and mops.

8:30pm

Dad's getting ready for work tomorrow. His first day. I've got all my stuff in my backpack, ready for Mere Park in the morning. Nat's mom is picking me up at nine. Mom's gone to bed early — she's really tired.

Chapter 20

<u>*Saturday, July 25th*</u>

Late. I don't know how late. I'm in my sleeping bag, lying on the trundle bed in my room. Nat's sleeping in my proper bed. I've got the little lamp on. I remembered that she doesn't like sleeping in the dark.

I can't believe it was only last night I wrote the last entry in my diary. What did I write — Oh, yes. *Mom's gone to bed early — she's really tired.* I didn't know *anything* when I wrote that.

I woke up early. Saturday morning. Going to Mere Park! That's the very first thought I had when I woke up. I jumped out of bed and pulled back the curtains. It was a perfect day. There wasn't any sun on our garden yet, but you could tell it was going to be hot because it was a little bit misty. High up, the sky was clear blue. Down on the grass there were blackbirds hopping about. One of them squinted up at the window, with his head on one side. He looked as if he was asking me what I was doing inside when it was so beautiful outside.

I'd be out there soon. I'd get dressed right away, have breakfast, get all my stuff ready, help Mom with the babies, make millions of bottles so she wouldn't have to make any during the day — and be all ready when Nat and her mom came to fetch me at nine o'clock.

But the bathroom door was locked. There was a horrible groaning sound coming through it. I didn't know what it was at first. Then suddenly I recognized the sound. Someone was being sick. Then Dad appeared behind me, his face creased up and anxious. He rattled the doorknob.

"Are you all right, Juliet? Open the door!"

More horrible sick sounds. Dad said to me: "She's been ill all night. She's been sick five times. I think it's food poisoning from that pork pie she had for dinner."

Mom is the only one of us who likes pork pies. She'd bought it as a treat for herself. The toilet flushed, we heard water running, then the lock clicked and Mom staggered out. Her face was grayish-white. Dad grabbed hold of her.

"Let's get you back to bed, love."

I took hold of Mom's other arm. She was burning hot. She didn't say anything, just collapsed onto the bed and lay there with her eyes shut, looking awful. "I'm so sorry," she whispered, and to my horror a tear slid out of the corner of one of her closed eyes, and began to trickle down her cheek.

"I'll get you some water," said Dad, and he dashed downstairs. I could hear the babies beginning to stir. I rushed downstairs after Dad to get the bottles ready.

Get the sterilized bottles out of the sterilizer, boil the water, let it cool, add the milk powder, cool the bottles a bit more, put the caps onto seal them if they're going in the fridge for later. I decided to make eight bottles, so the next feed would be ready for Mom. Still no crying yet. Dad came downstairs, rubbing his eyes and looking desperate.

"I can't leave her," he said. "I can't go to work. They'll understand, won't they?"

"But Dad — it's your first day. You've got to go in." I knew what would happen. He'd get the sack before he had even started. You can't phone and say you aren't coming, on your very first day at a new job.

"But what can I do?" Dad demanded. "She can't even stand up. How can she look after the babies?"

I took a deep breath. I thought of Mere Park and the beautiful summer day and the fabulous rides, and the fantastic picnic Nat had told me about, and the Cokes and cake in the café, and us buying souvenirs, and coming home late and tired and happy, laughing about nothing with Nat in the back of the car. Then I thought of Mom upstairs, looking as gray as death.

"I'll stay," I said. "I can manage. Maybe Mrs. Pearson could help me?"

"No," said Dad. "Mom says she's gone away to stay with her son for the weekend."

"Oh." I thought fast. Somebody else. Who? I knew I couldn't really manage four babies on my own, not unless I kept them in their cribs all day and just took them out one at a time for feeding and changing. But they'd hate that. They'd cry and cry, and Mom wouldn't be able to sleep.

Can't write any more now. Got to go to sleep . . .

Sunday, July 26th

It's quite early. Nat's still asleep. The babies are asleep, too. Only the birds are singing. The same blackbirds as yesterday.

Where was I? Oh yes, talking to Dad. Suddenly he turned to me, his face full of hope.

"Listen, Tanya. What about that friend of yours — Natalie? Could she come round and help?"

"I don't know. I could ask. I've got to phone her anyway, to tell her I can't come to Mere Park."

"It's only quarter-past seven," said Dad. "A bit early to ring."

"You get ready for work," I said firmly. "I'll ring Nat later." I could hear the babies starting to cry, so I grabbed a bunch of bottles and hurried upstairs.

Bottles, diapers, baby wipes, clean sleepers. The next

hour passed in a blur, with Dad and me working full speed. Luckily the beautiful morning seemed to have made the babies happy, too. They lay on their backs making little contented sounds and trying to roll over.

"I'll go and phone Nat now," I said, and ran downstairs.

Disaster. I got Nat's mom first. I started mumbling and apologizing, and she got icier and icier. She seemed to think I wasn't coming on purpose. As if I didn't want to come!

"Well, all I can say is that Natalie is going to be *very* disappointed. And at such short notice, too."

"Can I speak to her, please?"

"Well, I don't think — "

"*Please!*"

"Oh, all right then." She sounded so angry, as if I was an enemy. I heard her talking in the background for ages, then Nat came on the phone.

"Hello," she said, in a little flat voice. "Mom's told me. About you not coming."

"Nat. Listen. You *know* I want to come! The thing is, Mom's really sick and she can't look after the babies. I've got to stay at home. If Dad doesn't go to work he'll lose the job. You know, the one in the Chinese supermarket — I told you."

"I know," said Nat. Her voice sounded more normal. "I know it's not your fault, Tanya."

"Nat — do you think there's any chance your mom might

let you come round here? Just to give me a hand? I know she doesn't want you to do anything with the babies, but this *is* an emergency."

"I don't know," said Nat cautiously. "I could ask her."

"But would you come, if she let you?"

"Course I would!" said Nat. "I'd love to!" I was so surprised I nearly dropped the phone. *Love to?* She must be mad.

More background talk, going on for ages again. Dad was dancing around in the background tapping his watch to say *I've got to go soon.* Suddenly a voice crackled in my ear. It wasn't Nat, though. It was her mom, angrier than anyone had ever been with me before.

"I've had just about enough of this. How dare you spoil my Nat's day out, then ask her if she wants to come and do chores for you? I'd like to come round and tell your parents what I think of them!" I didn't know what to say. I held the phone away from my ear while her voice crackled on and on, then I just said, "Sorry, I've got to go now," and put it down.

"I've got to go in quarter of an hour," Dad was saying.

"I know. Wait. I'm going to ring Sushila."

Sushila was fantastic. I was only halfway through explaining what a massive favor I needed when she said, "I'll come. I'll check with Mom but I'm sure it'll be OK."

"Are you sure?"

"Course I'm sure! You're right. This is an emergency."

110

I put down the phone, slumped against the wall, and closed my eyes with relief. I opened them to find Dad staring at me anxiously.

"It's all right. You can go to work. Sushila's coming over," I said.

Dad raced up and down the stairs, talking to Mom, getting piles of diapers ready, giving me emergency phone numbers. I peeped in at Mom but she still had her eyes shut, so I tiptoed away. Dad helped me bring the babies downstairs, and put them in their bouncing cradles. He spread a big rug on the lawn.

"Sure you'll be OK, Tanya?"

"Sure," I said, much more surely than I felt. And then the door closed. I was alone with Sam and John, Jodie and Katie. Brother brother, sister sister. They looked at me expectantly, and then they smiled and kicked their legs.

Chapter 21

Four of them, and one of me. It was a bit scary. I decided to go and make more supplies of bottles while the babies were still happy. Just at that moment, the doorbell rang. It'd be Sushila! I rushed to answer it. I flung open the door saying, "Sushila! Oh, I'm so glad you've — "

Then I stopped. It wasn't Sushila. Nat stood there. Her fists were dug deep in her pockets and she was red with embarrassment.

"Nat!"

"Tanya, I'm so sorry, I'm so sorry about what my mom said."

"It doesn't matter. Come in. Or have you got to get back right away?"

"No," said Nat. "I'm staying. I've come to help you with the babies."

"You've — come to help me with the babies?" I repeated like an idiot.

"Yes."

"But — what about your mom?"

"She knows," said Nat grimly. "I told her I was coming and nothing she could do was going to stop me, except locking me in my room. And then I'd scream so all the neighbors could hear."

We were in the kitchen by then. The babies spotted Nat and started flapping their arms and waving their legs. Nat knelt down in front of the row of bouncy cradles.

"Hi," she said. "I'm Nat. I've come to help Tanya look after you. We're going to have a good time, aren't we?"

The babies flapped their arms even more and made happy crowing noises. Yes, they *did* think we were going to have a good time.

"What did your mom say then, after you told her you'd yell out of your bedroom window if she didn't let you come?" I asked.

"Nothing really," said Nat. "Well, she sat down on a chair and stared at me. Then she said, 'I can't stop you, I suppose.'"

"Wow. Imagine you saying all that."

"I know. I'd never have believed it. But I was just so angry when she was so horrible to you on the phone. I thought you'd never want to be my friend anymore."

I picked up Katie, who was squirming in a wet-diaper way. "Course I want to be your friend. Oh, there's the doorbell again. I bet that's Sushila."

It was Sushila. And not just Sushila. Rachel, too.

"I was going to play tennis with Rachel," Sushila

explained. "When I told her why I had to come to your house, she said she'd come, too."

Rachel smiled at me, a bit nervously.

"Four of us!" I said. "One for each baby. We'll be able to manage *everything*."

"Four?" asked Sushila, looking round.

"Yeah, Nat's here already," I said casually. "Come on in. The babies are with Nat in the kitchen."

I expect you think I'm going to say it was all easy from then on, don't you? No. Four babies are still four babies. And Sushila, Rachel, and Nat didn't know all that much about babies. They learned quickly, though. By the end of the day they knew how to change diapers, how to give a bottle, how to burp a baby, and how to sing *"Hush little baby, don't say a word, Mama's going to buy you a mockingbird,"* while bouncing a baby to sleep, without waking up any babies who were already asleep. This is what Mr. Cochrane calls "a steep learning curve." I kept having to rush upstairs to give Mom sips of water and help her to the bathroom.

But it was fun, too, in a way I'd never expected. After we'd had lunch (baked beans on toast) we all sat out in the garden with the babies. It was sunny but not too hot, and there was a breeze that kept the babies cool. We spread their rug in the shade, then we sprawled out on the grass while the babies kicked and looked up at the leaves. It was a beautiful day, just like I'd thought it was going to be when I woke up. But in every other way the day was the exact opposite of what I'd thought it would be. Nat was telling Rachel about skating because Rachel wants to learn. I was pulling the ends out of long pieces of grass and chewing them. Sush was playing *This Little Piggy* with Jodie's toes. I'd just been up to see Mom again, and she was fast asleep. Her face was still pale, but it wasn't gray any more. Dad phoned, and I told him everything was fine. Two o'clock. *Already he's earned sixty-five dollars,* I thought.

"You are lucky," said Nat, turning over onto her back and squinting at the sunlight.

"Lucky?"

"Oh, you know. Having brothers and sisters."

"But it's not really like having brothers and sisters," I said slowly. "I mean, they can't do anything. They're only babies."

"They won't *always* be babies," said Nat. "I still think you're lucky. Just think of being able to say, 'I've got two brothers and two sisters,' when people ask you about your family."

"Mm," I said doubtfully. Rachel didn't say anything. She's an only child, too. Sam was grunting and waving his arms frantically.

"Look!" said Nat. "He's trying to roll over onto his stomach."

"He can't do that yet," I said. Sam flapped and grunted. Suddenly, all at once, he rolled. His head turned, his arms waved. He rolled right over onto his stomach. Then he lifted up his head and beamed at us triumphantly.

"There you are," said Nat. "What did I tell you?"

I looked at the babies. I tried to imagine them doing the next thing, then the next. Crawling. Walking. Eating and drinking from plates and cups like real people. Talking. Running to the front door when I came home from school. Telling me stuff they'd been doing. And then all the bottles and diapers and screaming would be history. I imagined myself going to my new school in September, and people asking me about my family.

"Have you got any brothers and sisters, Tanya?"

"Yes. I've got two brothers, and two sisters. Sam and John, and Katie and Jodie."

Brother brother, sister sister. I say it in my head, and then I find I'm saying it out loud, though not too loud in case I wake Nat.

It sounds good.

P.S. I thought you might like to know about the extra pocket money. Five dollars a week! Not bad, is it? I'm going to save up, and then the next time Nat and I go to the movies, it won't be her mom paying. It'll be me.

About the Author

Helen Dunmore is an award-winning writer for both children and adults. She is a full-time writer, and works in a room at the top of her house where it is quiet (except when her four-year-old daughter comes to ask how she is doing).

Brother Brother, Sister Sister is her twenty-second book. She loves traveling, and her books are translated into many languages.